Unleashed Magic

Steve Higgs

To Barbara. R.I.P.

Contents

Chapter 1

January 2012. Bremen, Germany

Florian Hoss rarely went by his real name. He liked to think of himself as a shady character. He thought it made him sexy, and he certainly had a lot of women around him always trying to keep themselves in his good book. They weren't girlfriends though, they worked for him; they were his bitches.

That he was a pimp and a criminal wasn't something that played on his conscience. He liked what he did. He liked the power and being able to make his own rules. He made decent money too, and tonight had been a good night; takings amounted to almost a thousand Euros, a target he rarely reached. It was all profit too; he didn't share it with anyone. Most men in his line of work employed a heavy; someone who would deal with any problems, but even though he was both short and slight, he liked to think of himself as a hard man. He carried three knives and a gun just in case, but rarely had to use them. Producing a knife with the right attitude behind it did the trick most of the time.

He yawned. It was time to go home and get some sleep. Usually he would already be home in bed by now, but Magda had been late to return, her trick taking his time but paying well for the privilege. He had let Magda go with a warning, despite her earning more than anyone else tonight, but thinking about it now, he decided he probably needed to teach her a lesson anyway. Rules are rules after all.

His engine was running; it was far too cold to sit around without the heating on in his car, but he left the warmth to relieve himself in an alleyway, his need too pressing to drive home first.

Using a handy wall and gravity to do the work for him, he used both hands to take out a pack of smokes and light one. As he drew in a lungful of putrid air, a shadow crossed the mouth of the alleyway, catching his attention. He glanced up, just as he was about to put himself away and zip up. What he saw caused a double take and then the cigarette tumbled from his mouth.

Filling the mouth of the alley was a huge creature, its shoulders almost as wide as the gap between the buildings. Light glowed beneath its skin, somehow illuminating it from inside and it had to be at least two and a half metres tall. Florian registered all those details, but it was the rows of teeth beneath the red glowing eyes that held his attention.

'Hello,' it said.

His jaw twitched. He wanted to say hello in response, but he couldn't quite form the word. He wanted to believe it wasn't about to kill him, but the creature's arms ended with dagger-like claws that suggested otherwise. All he could do was look up at it, staring at the cloud of hot breath huffing out of its horrible mouth.

For the first time in years, he wanted to pray. He knew he was a bad person, not that it was something he ever really admitted to himself, but he knew it was true. Now he wanted to beg for forgiveness, to attend confession if that would save him from the monster blocking his escape route.

Suddenly, he remembered that he was armed. There was a knife in each front pocket and a gun tucked into the back of his jeans. What would a bullet do to this thing? He tried not to acknowledge what he was looking at, but his brain supplied a name for it anyway: werewolf.

The creature flexed its fingers slightly, the motion enough to break the spell that held Florian in place. He whipped his arm back to grab the gun, closed his hand around the pistol grip and yanked it free.

He always kept the safety on; he'd heard too many stories about guys shooting their junk off to risk putting it in his trousers loaded and live. It wouldn't have made any difference though, because he never had the time to bring the gun around.

The werewolf closed the distance to him in a heartbeat, raking Florian's chest with first one set of claws and then the next before shoving him roughly to the ground. Mercifully, Florian lost consciousness very quickly.

Chapter 2

The phone call came just as I was leaving the supermarket. Even though I now had little more than six days before I was due to surrender myself to Daniel the demon and become his familiar, I still needed to eat between now and then.

I fished my phone from my pocket, fumbling with car keys and trying to get my glove off because I couldn't swipe the screen to answer the call with it on. I answered, 'Otto Schneider, licensed detective.'

There were enough seconds of silence for me to pull the phone away from my ear to check the number and that it was still connected before trying again, 'Hello? This is Otto Schneider.'

'Herr Schneider, this is Chief Muller of the Bremen police. I'm sure you remember me.'

The instant answer on my lips was that my memory of our meeting was still quite fresh because he was such a dick at the time. I refrained from saying that though, curious to hear why he had chosen to call me. 'How can I help you, Chief Muller?'

There was another pause, the quiet at his end stretching on for a three-count before he said, 'I believe I may wish to hire you as a consultant on a case. Are you available?'

Chief Muller didn't ask if I was interested, maybe he assumed I was starving as a licensed detective and needed every case that came up. Or maybe he thought I would leap at the chance to work with the police. Neither was true but my interest was piqued enough to ask another question. 'What's the case?'

'Can you come to the station?'

'Why?' I was frowning at my phone and trying not to drop it as I placed the bags of shopping into the footwells in the rear of the car. I found my shopping always spilt in the boot of the car – any car, that is, but my wife's little silver 1961 Ferrari most especially.

'It is a delicate matter, Herr Schneider, I cannot talk about it over the phone.' His manner was gruff, he clearly expected compliance which was exactly the wrong approach to take with me.

'I have groceries to take home, Muller,' I hit his name hard when I said it, making sure he noticed me ignoring his rank; he wasn't the boss of me. 'I have too little time to have you wasting it for me.' With that, I joyously pressed the red button to end the call and put it back in my pocket.

I really was short on time, you see. My name is Otto Schneider and I am a wizard apparently. As a child, I considered there to be nothing special about me. I did all the normal things the other kids my age did: rode my bike, read comic books, tried to get into movies I wasn't old enough to see. At fourteen, all that changed. It wasn't a puberty thing, at least, I don't think it was. One day I woke up feeling tired like I did every other day as a teenager. School started at seven thirty and I had chores to do get done before I went, so my alarm went off at a quarter to six allowing me to get ready and leave by seven. It felt unfairly early even twenty years later. I remember a Tuesday, way back then, when I stared bleary-eyed into the mirror, it wobbled a bit. Not the mirror itself, just the reflection in it. I blinked, and that was the first time I brought up my second sight.

My reflection was shimmering with a golden haze. I later learned that what I could see was my magical aura but instead of freaking out, or being afraid, it actually made sense. My grandfather had been able to perform all kinds of cool magic tricks. He never did them when anyone else was around though, he only showed me. Often, he would say, 'Otto, my boy, one day you'll be able to do this too. This and so much more.' I had no idea what he was talking about and he died before I was ten, so I never got the chance to find out.

What he meant was that he could see in me what I was now seeing: magic. I could remember him making little eddies in a glass of water. He would hold his hand above the water and make it spin like a vortex. That was what I tried to do first. It was as if I could suddenly sense how the molecules of the earth were put together and what I needed to do to manipulate them. Moving water soon became forming water, taking tiny atoms of moisture from the air to coalesce them into droplets. I could literally make it rain. Next it was air, using magic to create eddies in the air like small tornadoes in the palm of my hand.

I knew it was amateur stuff, and each new thing I tried to learn took months of persistent effort to gain any control. I was learning though and once I could do one thing, more and more doors opened. By the time I left school at eighteen, I had amassed a set of skills that would allow me to conjure fire and lightning, to control water and air and to be able to move the very ground beneath my feet. Over the years, I added more spells to my repertoire: a tracking spell which allowed me to find lost people or animals and a protective spell that created a barrier of energy I could hide behind.

What was I though? I had no frame of reference other than the comic books and films I grew up on. Wizards and magic weren't real, everyone knew that. They were just fictional notions. Except... except I could do magic.

The tracking spell, among other things, had formed the basis of my professional career – I found missing persons. By my late twenties, I was a licenced private detective. I had a high success rate because of another odd quirk, one that allowed me to know if a person was lying or not. Question enough people connected to a crime and sooner or later you will find the person that is lying about their part in it. Missing persons was the most rewarding part of my job but came at a cost. Finding a kidnapped child or a runaway teenager was always heart-warming, when I found them still alive. The spell told me where they were, not what condition they were in.

I'm thirty-four now, which means teenagers think I am an old man. I still feel young and still exercise regularly but I doubted I was going to bother with any of that this week because it was to be my last week on Earth. At some point early this morning, somewhere around four o'clock I thought, I agreed to bind myself to a demon called Daniel. The last few days had been a little hectic, shall we say. The result of it all was a fight with another demon, this one called Teague, in a realm I could only access through a portal I could not conjure for myself. I went there to save some people and to find out what the hell was going on in my home town of Bremen. I fought, I won (sort of), but to get home I had to agree to become Daniel's familiar, a position I wasn't, ahem, familiar with, so had no real idea what that might entail.

It was nothing good, I knew that much. So, with a little more than six days left to go until I was taken away from Earth, I was acting as if I was dying and had gone to the supermarket to buy all the things I wouldn't normally allow myself. The list started with a thirty-five-year-old single malt scotch whisky, moved swiftly to half litre tubs of the best ice cream in the shop and didn't stop there.

As the engine caught and leapt into life with a roar, my phone rang again. I harrumphed, told myself to ignore it, then answered it anyway because I knew going home to get drunk and uncomfortably fat by myself was a bad idea.

'There has been a murder,' said Chief Muller. 'The circumstances are... strange.'

'How strange?' I asked, frowning to myself in the darkness of the car.

He snorted. 'Strange enough for me to call you, Schneider.'

Okay, fair point.

'It's not the first one,' he admitted, sensing my resolve wavering and casting a fresh hook. I was probably mixing my metaphors, but he had me either way.

'I have frozen goods in the car. I need to get them home first.'

He snorted again. 'Herr Schneider, it's minus four outside. Nothing is going to defrost this side of March.'

Accepting defeat, I opened my mouth to tell him I would be there in twenty minutes, the time it would take to get between the two points, but then I thought of something. 'What is the current status of Detective Lieutenant Heike Dressler?'

'She's on suspension. You know that.'

'Not anymore. If you want me, that is my price. I won't charge a fee if I work with her.'

'I suspended her, Schneider,' he argued. 'I can't just reinstate her, there's a hearing in two days' time to decide her fate.'

'You have my terms, Muller. Both of us, or neither. Keep her on suspension and hire her in as a special consultant if you have to. I don't care about the details. Officer Nieswand is back, yes?'

Begrudgingly he said, 'Yes.'

'That's because of her actions.'

'She got another officer killed.' This time he raised his voice to drive the point home.

'That's a pile of crap and you know it. Prochnow got killed because no one, most especially you, would listen to me. The strange stuff then is the same strange stuff now. You are just getting used to the idea, that's all. That's why you called me. I'll be there in twenty minutes. If I haven't heard from Dressler by then, I won't even stop the car.' I jabbed the red button to end the call and put the phone on the passenger's seat.

I recognised that my sense of victory was juvenile, but I let myself bask in it anyway. Heat was coming through the air vents now to thaw my fingers and toes so I cupped my hands around one of them for a few seconds, hoping Heike would call before I set off. My wife's vintage car didn't have hands free, Bluetooth stuff, so to answer a call I would have to pull over. In the early evening city traffic, that might not be easy.

Nothing happened though, the phone ignoring my wishes as it silently mocked me. I put the car in gear and set off. What I should have done was go home and open the whisky; I would have saved myself a lot of heartache, bruises and trouble if I had.

Chapter 3

The call from Heike came just as I turned into the street with the police station on it. I meant what I said about not stopping if I hadn't heard from her, so I wasn't bothering to look for a place to park. I wanted to answer the phone but right outside a police station was not the place to chance using a phone while driving.

My rear-view mirror had a set of headlights in it and there looked to be more behind that so my thought of just stopping to answer the phone got dismissed also. There were spaces on the other side of the street, but I would have to go to a junction and turn around or maybe circle a block to get back there now.

The phone stopped ringing. I had missed the call. A few seconds later, just as I was turning around to head back, the phone beeped with an incoming voice message and I stabbed the button quickly to hear it.

The phone beeped as it started playback. 'Otto, this is Heike. I got a call from Muller. Something you did got me temporarily reinstated, you complete dick. I was going to have a few days off, but now, apparently, I am on a case and you are my special consultant. Next time phone a person.' The message clicked off.

I screwed up my face as I tried to work out if she had been joking or not. I didn't know her very well. We met for the first time a few days ago but I had the impression she was a dedicated career police officer with an eye on one of the top spots. Surely, she would be jumping at the chance to get stuck back in after being so wrongly suspended. Maybe she thought it would all get cleared up at her hearing later this week, and therefore, she could get away with doing nothing for a few days and come out smelling of roses.

I wasn't sure. She would be on her way to the station though so I would find out soon enough.

With the car backed into a parking spot, I crossed the street and ran up the steps to the police station's main reception. I wasn't made to wait long, Officer Klaus Nieswand appeared to fetch me in under five minutes. I was surprised to see him working; only yesterday he had been held captive in the immortal realm where he was to be sold to a demon to act as its familiar.

'I couldn't stand being at home by myself,' he admitted. 'I'm still a little freaked out by it all. I have no magical powers,' he dropped his voice for the last sentence, 'so, I probably would have ended up dead, discarded when they realised I was no use to them.'

I said nothing. It was my theory that Daniel was grabbing anyone who showed signs of being able to wield elemental magic; basically, anyone with an aura. He took them, tested them, tried to train them so they could be of use as a familiar to a demon and then, if they genuinely had no ability, he would kill them and dump them back on Earth. Officer Nieswand might well have been one of those discarded victims, though one had to question which fate was worse.

He led me through a wide, open-plan office where dozens of cops were working at desks. Some in uniform, still wearing all their gear having only just come in or getting ready to go out, and some stripped down because it was warm in the office. Others were in plain clothes, cheap suits mostly.

'We call this the pit,' he explained as we followed a path between the desks. Several pairs of eyes tracked us, or more accurately, me, as I was the unknown entity, but most didn't bother to look up.

Through the pit, he pushed open a door, which led into a corridor. At the end of the corridor, which had doors coming off to the left and the right, there was another door facing us. That's where we went.

Inside, the first person I saw was Detective Sergeant Schenk, a burly bear of a man who didn't like me and was quite happy to show it. He must have known I was coming because he didn't question my arrival, only turning to give me his back, clearly under the delusion that I might want to see his face.

Nieswand steered me toward Chief Muller whose back was also to me as he and two others were hunched over a table.

'Chief,' Nieswand prompted.

Chief Muller had been rude and unpleasant when we last spoke face to face and every time we spoke before that. There had long been rumours about me. I was one of only two licensed detectives in Bremen and the job brought me into semi-regular contact with the cops. I had been spotted performing spells once or twice, though to the casual observer I just looked like I was doing something strange with a wand. I had also made the mistake of telling people the truth a few times in the past; yes, magic exists. So, the chief had always viewed me as a charlatan even though I was well-known for finding missing persons and solving cases the police hadn't been able to. This wasn't a missing person case though; it was a murder. He had already told me that, so his decision to call me in had to mean he was coming to accept that the recent spate of deaths in Bremen and the reports of strange occurrences by his own officers, had to mean I wasn't making all of it up.

I already decided on the way over that I wasn't going to bother hiding my nature anymore. Heike and Klaus Nieswand had seen it already and they weren't the only ones, plus with less than a week left on Earth, what did it matter now?

Through the gaps between the people now turning to face me, I could see photographs of a person lying in the snow. Each of the pictures contained far more red than they ought to.

Chief Muller offered his hand to shake, which I took, trying to start off on the right foot this time. He said, 'Thank you for coming so quickly, Herr Schneider. Can I call you Otto? Herr Schneider will get boring after a while.'

'Sure.' I let go of his hand and let him introduce the other members of his team.

'You already know Detective Sergeant Schenk. He will be leading this team as one of my most senior detectives. Joining him is Officer Nieswand, who volunteered despite being signed off from work.' He clapped Nieswand on the shoulder as a gesture of acknowledgement for his dedication.

A man in his late thirties, who had been talking quietly on the phone when I came in, now shoved his way into the crowd and stuck out his hand before the chief could move onto the next person. 'I'm Special Investigator Voss of the Deutsche Kriminal Investigation Bureau. I believe you have already met my boss, Deputy Commissioner Bliebtreu.' I took his hand because it was right there but didn't comment on his rudeness. I had met his boss, so I knew the Kriminal Investigation Bureau name was nothing more than a cover story. They were the Supernatural Investigation Alliance. That's what Bliebtreu told me and he was telling the truth about their intention to prepare for whatever was coming. Voss added, 'I'm here to liaise should it be necessary.'

Now I was curious. 'Liaise how exactly?'

'Our remit is to assist municipal police services when they face cases of an... unusual nature. The frequency of such cases is increasing and the danger from them also. I am here merely to observe at this time. The Bremen police will be handling the investigation but should the current murder enquiry prove to have an... unusual element,' he said, choosing his words carefully, 'then I will deploy forces to assist.'

'Assist?' questioned the chief. 'You took over last time and that was just a few days ago. How did you even know about this case? You arrived from Berlin within an hour of the body being discovered.'

Voss turned his attention to the older man. 'Yes. The previous Deputy Commissioner had distinct ideas about how he wanted the Bureau to operate. With Deputy Commissioner Bliebtreu at the helm, you will find us more cooperative. How the Bureau knew about the case is unimportant at this time.'

The chief held his gaze for a while, not offering an argument, not disagreeing, but looking for signs in the man's eyes that might indicate how much truth was in his words. I could tell that he wasn't lying. Well, apart from the bit about the name of his organisation, but his claim to be cooperative was genuine.

I asked, 'Where are the rest of the Bureau's men?'

My question broke the staring contest between Voss and Muller, the chief turning away from the younger man and looking about for his mug of coffee to pick it up for a slurp as he said, 'They all left this morning. Not long after you... returned, actually.' My memory flashed back to my conversation with Bliebtreu. He said he believed me when I claimed the danger here was past. I wasn't convinced he would act on it, but perhaps he was good to his word after all.

The interlude with Voss now done, Chief Muller got back to making introductions. There were just two people left. 'These are Detectives Rugler and Moltz.' Rugler and Moltz were both around thirty and would make an attractive couple if they got together. Rugler was lean and athletic, a natural blonde with straight hair pulled into a tidy ponytail. She had high cheek bones and dark eyes that reminded me of a Latin American actress whose name or films I couldn't remember. At around a metre seventy-five Rugler would be taller than an average man if she put on heels. Next to her, Moltz stood a metre ninety tall, allowing him to look me directly in the eye. His dark hair was styled upward into short spikes and he was broad and muscular like a professional sportsman. Both wore smart casual office wear. I shook each of their hands in turn and asked their first names. Corinna and Christoph ought to be easy to remember but my attention was already being lost to the pictures on the table.

'May I?' I asked, wanting to get a closer look, my way blocked by Moltz and Rugler.

The chief stepped out of the way. 'Of course. That's what you're here for.' Moltz and Rugler realised they too were in the way and stepped politely to the side. So far, the team, with the exception of Schenk, seemed receptive.

The photographs had been printed rather than displayed on a screen, most likely because it was easier to look at several of them at once this way; looking at multiple pics on a single computer screen made each one smaller.

They were gruesome. That was the standout factor my brain registered first. A man in his forties had been shredded and left to ooze his vital fluids into the snow. Dressed for the weather, his clothes were nevertheless torn open to show how much damage had been done to his internal organs. Most of them looked to be missing. I fanned out a few more pictures.

His glassy eyes stared to the night sky, his body illuminated by lights erected so the police could record the details and see what they were doing. The feet of tripods snuck their way into some of the pictures, the large lights shining down from their high reach.

The man had tattoos on his neck and his teeth were yellowed from smoking. He hadn't looked after himself; he looked malnourished in fact; his face almost gaunt. I sucked in a deep breath through my nose, exhaling again as I stood back from the table.

'What can you tell me?' I asked.

It was Rugler that answered, 'His name is Florian Hoss. Forty-three years old, from Croatia. Arrested seven times in the last ten years, always in connection with running prostitutes. He was robbed as well as being gutted.'

'Robbed?' I queried. 'Is that important?'

It was Moltz who answered, 'We don't know yet. If robbery was the motivation and they killed him to stop him identifying them, then the injuries he sustained defy explanation. Kill him, but don't tear him apart.'

'What was taken?' I asked.

'Whatever was in his wallet. We interviewed some of the girls he runs... ran. It was late so they had been working and had already handed over their takings for the night. Watch and rings were taken as well. In fact, the killer took everything but his phone.'

Rugler said, 'The robbery sounds opportunistic. Like the point of this was murder, but then there's a wallet full of money on the ground so the killer decided to take it.'

I looked at the officers facing me. 'Is this the first murder like this?'

'Yes,' said Chief Muller. 'Though we are reaching out nationally and across Europe to see if there have been any cases like this in the last ten years. Have you ever seen anything like this before?'

My forehead creased as I tried to work out why I had been called in. I specialised in finding missing people, it was a profession that lent itself well to my particular set of skills, yet here I was being shown the crime scene photographs from a very gruesome murder. Before I could answer his question or ask one of my own, the door opened behind me.

We all looked, the cops turning their heads to see while I had to turn through one hundred and eighty degrees. Coming through the door was Heike Dressler, currently back from suspension though technically still suspended. She didn't wave, not at anyone. She didn't slow her pace either, letting the door shut itself as she crossed the room. Detective Lieutenant Heike Dressler is a mother of four in her later thirties and a career police officer. She married a successful dentist with his own practice so wasn't doing the job for the money. A little spreading and softening had occurred from the multiple pregnancies; it set her apart from women like Corinna Rugler, who was only a handful of years younger but still firm and appealing. Basically, Heike looked like a mum, with her sensible clothes and sensible shoes and sensible shortish brown hair. She didn't wear much makeup, but she was a ballbuster and wasn't going to take crap from anyone.

'What have we got?' she asked. I stepped to the side so she could see the photographs. They told the picture better than I could articulate it. We were all silent for a few seconds while she inspected them. 'Anything back from the crime scene guys yet?'

Mugler said, 'No. Preliminary findings and speculation from the scene but you know what they are like...'

'No commitment until they can scientifically prove their findings,' Moltz finished her sentence.

'It looks like an animal attack,' Heike concluded.

The chief snorted in a huffing, angry way, 'It looks like a shark attack.'

Heike looked at me, searching my eyes for agreement to a question she hadn't asked. I offered her none, but she didn't really need it; she already knew what she was looking at. 'I've seen wounds like this before,' she announced. I closed my eyes and wished it wasn't true. 'You are going to have to suspend your disbelief for a moment, ok?'

Chief Muller frowned at her, Moltz and Rugler gave her curious looks and Schenk just leaned against a wall looking angry.

Holding centre stage, Heike said, 'These look like wounds inflicted by a werewolf.'

Schenk burst out laughing. 'A werewolf,' he snorted.

'It's true, man,' argued Nieswand. 'I saw one. It was huge and deadly. Its claws looked like they could cut through steel.'

Forcibly maintaining his mirth, Schenk challenged him, 'How come you survived then?'

Now Nieswand's face coloured when he said, 'It was friendly.'

Schenk's guffaw was enough to be too much for me. I arrived tonight expecting to find myself at this point sooner or later. With Schenk involved, I should be surprised that it wasn't sooner. I pushed flame into my right hand, drawing on ley line energy in the earth beneath the station to conjure the spell. It flickered and danced in my palm.

Moltz and Rugler stepped back in surprise. Even the chief's eyebrows shifted up his forehead, but he was too worn down by years as a cop to let me visibly shake him.

Now that I had everyone's undivided attention, I made eye contact with each of them, taking my time to lock eyes before moving on to the next person. 'If you don't believe in the supernatural, you might as well leave now.' No one said anything but I could see the barely contained anger brimming behind Schenk's eyes. I took a pace toward him. 'What do you think kidnapped Nieswand the other night? What do you think killed Prochnow? There are things happening that even I cannot explain but how many eyewitness reports will you ignore before you have to accept the inevitable?' I doused my spell and summoned moisture, pulling it into a cloud which then began to rain half a metre above Schenk's head.

Seething with anger, but with nothing he could say in response, he turned on his heel and stormed from the room. The door slammed hard, rattling the frame and the wall.

'He's a good detective,' said Chief Muller.

'We don't need him,' replied Heike, dismissing Schenk and turning back to the pictures. 'Could it be *him*?' she asked, the question aimed at me even though she didn't say it was.

I sighed. 'I don't know him any better than you do. I met him hours before we found you in the woods.'

'Who are we talking about?' the chief demanded to know.

I sighed again. 'I met a man in Berlin when I was taken there by the Bureau.' I left out the bit about them kidnapping me. 'He turned out to be a shapeshifter.' I saw their faces. 'Someone who can change forms. He is a big man, over two metres tall and very muscular. In his werewolf form he could easily inflict wounds like these, but I don't think he's the guy responsible.'

'Why not?' asked Rugler.

'Because he was all about helping people. I got the impression he keeps to himself and he had a distinct sense of right and wrong.'

'Sounds like a vigilante to me,' argued Moltz. 'Exactly the kind of guy to attack a pimp.'

The chief was getting interested. 'That sounds like our guy.'

'And he was in Bremen last night,' added Heike.

'Because he had just finished rescuing you,' I pointed out. I wasn't happy about the guilty conclusion being drawn so swiftly. I didn't see him as a killer. 'What time was Hoss killed?'

'Somewhere about six this morning,' supplied Moltz.

Dammit, the timings lined up. 'That's doesn't make him guilty, Heike.'

She countered my argument instantly. 'But it does make him a suspect and highly worthy of questioning.'

'What's his name?' asked Moltz, sliding into a chair positioned in front of a computer.

I didn't answer, which made everyone look my way. 'He just saved a dozen lives,' I protested. 'Yours included,' I added, jabbing a finger at Heike.

She nodded, her face sympathetic. 'We need to rule him out, Otto. We don't know enough about him to discount him from the investigation.' She held up a photograph of the dead man, forcing me to look away. 'If he didn't do it, he may be able to assist us. If this is a werewolf attack, he could be the key to finding the killer.'

She had me there and she knew it. 'Zachary Barnabus,' I supplied, loud enough for Moltz to hear. 'He's Hungarian. Or, at least, he said he was Hungarian.' It felt like a betrayal; I doubted I could have survived the previous day without him by my side and he had come with me willingly. I couldn't even remember asking him to for that matter. He just accepted that there were people to help and put his life on the line to rescue them. Those were not the actions of a person who then tore a man apart a few hours later.

At the computer terminal, Moltz let out a low whistle, the kind a person makes when they see something impressive. 'He's got quite the record.' Chief Muller, Heike, Rugler, and Nieswand were already moving in his direction when he spoke, his whistle enough to draw them. I went too, though there were too many people crowded around the computer already for me to be able to see anything.

Heike read from the screen. 'Assault, bodily harm, assault.' She didn't read the whole list; it was too long. 'It's all violent crime. Some suggested use of weapons, but having seen his alternate form, he could have used a claw.'

Moltz tapped the screen with a fingernail, getting eyes to track to the section he was looking at. 'There's an outstanding warrant for his arrest in Bulgaria.'

'Then we need to pick him up anyway,' said the chief, standing upright again having seen enough to be convinced. 'Nieswand, get an APB out with his photograph and description. Arrest on sight, consider extremely dangerous. Make sure it is circulated nationally.'

Nieswand scurried away, obediently performing the order.

Muller turned his attention to me. 'Do you have a number for him?'

'No.' I shook my head. 'I don't think he's the kind of guy that exchanges numbers. I have no expectation of ever seeing him again.'

The chief moved to an interactive screen and pulled Zachary's photograph onto it, drew a line and wrote suspect number one with a light pen. He stared at the screen, but over his shoulder he said, 'Heike I want you to assist Schenk on this case. You cannot lead it until you are reinstated.'

'He's not even here, chief,' she pointed out.

'He'll come around. He's a good detective.' It wasn't the first time he had made that claim, yet I saw no evidence of its truth.

I checked my watch: It was time for me to go. I was going to visit my wife in the hospital, and nothing was going to stop me. Touching Heike's arm, I kept my voice quiet when I said, 'I have to go. I can be available later.' When she looked up at me, I added, 'It's not him, you know. This is the work of someone else.'

She nodded but she said, 'We don't know that for certain. Until we do, we have to proceed cautiously.'

'He said he was leaving the city.'

'Then I hope he did, but what I really hope is that we can catch the monster that did this.' There was nothing I could think of to say in response. She was right that we needed to catch the killer, so I let it go, taking my leave as I let Rugler escort me back to the station's reception area.

Outside, I pulled my coat tight around me as the cold night air bit. If I had been more cautious, I might have raised my second sight and seen that I was being watched.

Chapter 4

Nine months ago, I returned home from work to find a man standing in my kitchen. The man wore a black silk shirt and black trousers, his dark brown, almost black, hair was cut short at the back and sides and he had a trimmed beard that was little more than a two-week stubble. The standout feature, the thing I saw first and would always remember, was his piercing blue eyes.

Staring across my kitchen at him, I barely had time to register my surprise before I saw my wife lying on the kitchen tile near his feet. She looked unconscious, but as my surprise turned to fear and anger, the man moved his left hand, creating a shimmering pool of air behind him. He stepped through it and vanished, the pool's circumference diminishing to nothing until it disappeared with a barely audible pop half a second later.

I spent weeks trying to understand what I had seen. The man had vanished right in front of me. In all my life, I had never seen another supernatural creature until that day. I wanted to find him, to find out what he had been doing in my house that day, but I had no starting point from which to begin a search. Then, just a couple of days ago, I heard another person describe the same piercing blue eyes and just this morning, I met him.

His name is Daniel, and he is a demon.

Thinking back to that fateful night, I shuddered. Kerstin, my wife of seven years, had a lump on her skull which turned out to be an impact wound. The police said it was almost certainly the case that she hit her head on the edge of the kitchen counter; they found blood, hair and tissue there. Her brain swelled from the injury and they had to cut her skull open to relieve the pressure. Her operation and treatment, whether she would survive the first twenty-four hours, all happened while the police interviewed me. I didn't tell them about the man. How could I? if I told them he was in my house, I would then have to explain how he got away, so I lied and said I came home to find her on the floor.

They kept going over and over the questions. I was lying about the detail and they knew it. They assumed domestic violence and I couldn't blame them for reaching such an obvious conclusion, but it didn't change that I was innocent and that I wanted to see my wife. In the end, it was a lack of evidence that got me released; no other marks on her body from previous abuse, no wound from a blow that I might have inflicted to knock her over.

The doctors told me she was in coma but that she was past the worst danger. They would monitor her and keep her body as healthy as they could. She could wake up at any time. She might never wake up ever again.

I visited her every night. My beautiful wife.

The last two nights I hadn't managed my usual two to three hours at her bedside. The first night I had found myself locked in a cell after the Bureau, who I now knew as the Alliance, thought it safer for them if they locked me up. Last night I missed my bedside appointment because I was fighting wizards, demons, and other creatures in a parallel realm. I told her all about it tonight while I held her hand. I told her about the way my magic had changed when they took away my wand and I discovered I didn't need it after all. For decades it had been my tool to focus my spells. Age improved my focus naturally though, so without it, I was stronger, and the change in what I could do was startling. I told her about Zachary the shifter, about meeting him in the cell block in Berlin and about how freakishly big he was. I didn't tell her about the murdered man in the snow and I didn't tell her that to get Katja and Heike back home I had to agree to become a demon's familiar. It meant I wouldn't... actually I had to concede that I didn't know what it meant. Convinced it was something negative, all my thoughts regarding the arrangement were depressing. I didn't know if I would be able to come back to visit Kerstin. But it felt like a safe assumption. I would be Daniel's slave or something akin to it. Bound to him in a way that would make me do his bidding unless I could find a way to prevent that from happening.

Silence ruled in her room while I held her hand and wallowed in my own depressing thoughts. Would I be forced to perform despicable tasks for him? What would happen when I refused?

A noise in the hallway snapped me back to reality and I realised I had dozed off with my head on her bed. 'Ten minutes, Herr Schneider,' called the voice of a nurse on his way by. I got to know the staff here by name over the course of the last nine months but hadn't seen his face to know which of them had spoken to me. Probably Thomas I decided, kissing Kerstin's hand as I got up and gathered my things.

My head swam as I stood upright, forcing me to duck down again until it passed. The second attempt went a little better, but I didn't feel right. Had I caught a cold? I shook it off; there was no time for such indulgences. It was late and though I already slept for a good portion of the day, I was ready for my bed. Tomorrow, I would do what I could with the police to find the killer.

Chapter 5

I awoke to an insistent hammering noise, finding myself disorientated as the dream I had been lost in slipped away to nothingness. There was someone at my door, the message finally forging a path through the fug of my brain to get my feet moving.

I felt terrible. Snagging a robe from my bedroom door as I stumbled and staggered out to find who was there, I added up all the different bits of me that were currently complaining. My kidneys ached, I felt cold, my ears felt like I was underwater. The list went on and all I wanted to do was go back to bed.

The shadow behind the door was Heike Dressler, who thrust her way into my house the moment the door started to open.

'What's going on, Otto? It's almost noon. I've been phoning you for hours.' I stumbled backward out of her way as she barrelled past, pushing the door shut again quickly as the cold air outside bit at my exposed skin. 'God are you alright, Otto?' she asked as she got a proper look at me. 'You look terrible.'

'Thank you, Heike. So good to see you.' I found myself squinting at the clock on the wall opposite. She was right: it was close to noon which meant I had been asleep for close to twelve hours, something I hadn't done in decades. 'I think I might be coming down with something.'

Cautiously, Heike asked, 'Are you too sick to work?'

I shook my head, trying to clear it as well as answering her question. 'I'll be fine. I just woke up, that's all. Let me get some clothes and get a cup of coffee into me...'

As I went one way, back toward my bedroom, Heike went the other, heading for the kitchen. 'I'll get the coffee going.'

I figured she could manage that task without involving me or ever having been in my kitchen before. Which, of course, proved to be true as the scent of coffee caught my nose a few minutes later once I was dressed and heading to the kitchen myself.

The mirror in my bathroom hadn't been filled with good news. I looked as bad as I felt: red-rimmed eyes with dark bags beneath them despite the many hours of sleep. It was all minor ailments and certainly nothing more than a winter cold, yet it was the worst cold I believed I had ever experienced.

Coming into the kitchen, I saw Heike with a cup of coffee under her nose as she blew over the surface to cool it. Steam rose from a second cup on the counter, but it wasn't what I expected. 'Your machine is too complex,' she explained. 'I found instant in the cupboard.'

'Really?' I asked, surprised there was instant coffee in the house.

Heike put her cup down and leaned a hip against the counter. 'There was another murder this morning.' It wasn't welcome news. 'Just like the last, another man left to bleed into the snow. Another criminal lowlife involved in the sex industry. This time it was a man that runs a titty bar we believe runs prostitutes on the side.'

'Have you been to the scene?'

'Since they called me at ten to five this morning. They called you too.'

I sighed, looking around. 'I'm not even sure where my phone is.'

Heike picked up her coffee and took a swig from the cup. I grabbed mine too, wanting the better stuff, the dark, strong, elegant blend my machine could produce, but it was made now, and it would be impolite to pour it away. Mercifully, the face I pulled as the sour flavour invaded my taste buds was mimicked by hers. 'God that's awful,' she shuddered, moving to the sink to dispose of it.

'I'll make it,' I volunteered. 'You can tell me all about the second victim while it brews.'

A knock at my door interrupted me just as I was getting the beans out to grind. Tutting, because I wanted to get the machine going before I answered it, Heike saw my face twitch. 'I'll get it,' she announced as she left the kitchen.

My kitchen sits at the end of my living space which is a long room incorporating my dining room and lounge area. It is accessed immediately one comes through the front door although it sits half a metre and three steps above a small lobby area. It is close enough that I could hear Heike talking to someone but not so close that I could hear what was being said. When she reappeared a few minutes later, she had an official looking envelope; the type that one must sign for.

'It's a court summons,' she told me. I made a surprised face, to which she added, 'You're being sued.'

I could have worked that out for myself, but I had no idea who might wish to pursue me for damages. The answer was easy to find though. When I opened the envelope, the document inside bore the name of a well-known local law firm and their client: Herr Karl Weber.

'That was swift,' Heike observed. 'I guess he didn't like your display the other night.'

Two nights ago, I returned a fifteen-year-old girl to her parents and got into a fight with the father because he is an arrogant dick. He wanted me to explain what had happened but refused to believe a supernatural explanation. So, I used a spell to lift him from the floor and made him crap his pants. Now he wanted to get revenge.

I continued reading, looking for pertinent information. 'They want an initial meeting next week.' I couldn't help but to snort with derision. 'Good luck making me attend that.' I was going to be the slave of a demon by then.

Heike touched my arm. 'What are you going to do about that, Otto? You can't let Daniel take you.'

'Can't I? I don't see how I can stop him.' The coffee machine finished its cycle, dispensing an unctuous thick espresso. I set it to make another for myself and turned to look at Heike. 'He is more powerful than me, by quite a margin, I suspect, but the bigger problem is that I already agreed to his terms and he will rain fire and destruction on Bremen if I do not. That was his promise and I see no easy way of preventing it. He could go after Katja again. He could swamp the place in shilt. If I am there, perhaps I can control him a little.'

She clearly wasn't happy with the concept and was going to present some kind of argument any second now. I got in first. 'I think we should focus on the murders here. What can you tell me about the second murder?'

'Well, it wasn't the second. That's the new development. When the chief reached out, he found there were others like it in the recent weeks. They started in the Czech Republic sixteen days ago in a small village not far from Brno.'

'What's there?'

'Nothing. It's a small village, population of less than five hundred. There's farmland and very little else. Moltz and Rugler were looking into it, but they already reported that a girl went missing at the same time. The victim was her uncle, local law enforcement assume she is also dead, and her body is yet to be discovered.'

'Tell me about the other murders.'

She knocked back her espresso in one hit, causing me to do the same. The harshness of the caffeine would do wonders for my alertness; dulled by my cold, I needed a pick me up. 'We think there have been four in total. The two here in the last two nights, one near Brno, possibly the girl of course but we won't count that until we find a body and one in a town just outside of Leipzig.'

'Were any during the period that Zachary was held by the Alliance?'

She pursed her lips and shook her head slowly back and forth. She was sorry, but he was still firmly on the suspects list. A list that currently had only one name on it. 'What do you make of Voss?' she asked unexpectedly.

I thought about my answer before I gave it. 'I found Deputy Commissioner Bliebtreu in my house when I got home yesterday morning.'

'He broke in?' she questioned.

'Nothing broken, but essentially... yes. He wanted to advise me that he had taken over from Schmidt, the chap that had me taken captive and held without due process. I think they are operating under some kind of terrorist law subset where they can make people vanish if they feel the need. They also had scientists who were doing stuff to a pair of shilt they had in a basement.'

'Doing stuff?'

'Experiments, I guess. Bliebtreu told me the Alliance is linking up with other nations as they try to work out why the occurrence of supernatural events is increasing. They want to be able to fight back so they need information. How many creatures are we facing? What can they do? What do we have to do to stop them? The shilt can be killed by bullets, we have proven that; they bleed and die like any creature, but it is not as simple as shooting at them because their reflexes are so fast, they are able to deflect the bullets. Bullets wouldn't work on a demon though; they claim to be immortal and I don't think it's just good marketing. I'm not sure what a bullet would do to Zachary either. Probably just piss him off. You had gone through the portal already when Daniel spoke to him, but he expected Zachary to die when he hit him with... what did he call it?' I wracked my brain for a moment before the term popped up. 'Oh, yes, hell fire. That's what he said the red balls of light from his hands were called. He seemed quite put out that Zachary survived.'

My memory flashed to the scene. We found ourselves in a demon's house. It was night and we were there to rescue Katja Weber, a terrified teenage girl taken from her home by Daniel to be traded as a familiar for favour. The demon had other ideas though, fighting back and proving the claim to be immortal when I exploded every cell in his body and he started to magically reform. Daniel showed up and offered me a deal I had to accept in order to save the others. Teague, the demon whose house we invaded, was about to recover and I had no fight left in me for another round. I was outgunned, outnumbered, and out of options. We survived, but we shouldn't have, Zachary most especially according to Daniel and that made me question just how tough the werewolf was.

'Otto!' I snapped my head around to look at Heike. 'Otto, I have been talking to you for the last minute and getting no response. Where were you?'

'Sorry,' I mumbled. 'I drifted off. What were you saying?'

Heike tried again. 'You think the Alliance are rounding up supernatural creatures to perform experiments on them?'

I shrugged. 'I wouldn't say that I approve. Especially since they most likely see me as a supernatural myself. I think Schmidt saw me flinging spells around and concocted a reason to take me captive right there and then. I guess it makes sense though.' She didn't like that, and I felt I needed to defend myself. 'Like I said, I'm not approving it, but if it is a werewolf killing people, don't you think it would be a good idea to know how to stop it?'

Heike pushed off the counter with her hip where she was still leaning against it. 'We should get to the station. There is evidence to look at and we need to liaise with the team or risk overlapping tasks.'

I moved to follow her, but my head swam again like it had when I first got out of bed. I stumbled in the kitchen doorway like a drunk man, grabbing the frame for support. Through a fog I could hear Heike talking to me, but the words were lost. There was a sense of otherness, like I was here but I was also somewhere else. The best way I could describe it was like seeing one scene with one eye and a totally different scene with another. Both scenes were hitting my brain simultaneously and it couldn't cope. I thought about vomiting, the sharp taste of bile filling my throat, but I bit it back as I wrestled for control. Shutting both eyes made little difference but bringing up my second sight did. As I opened my eyes with the supernatural filter on, I saw the aura of supernatural creatures through my left eye. I scrambled backward in panic, falling on my butt in the kitchen doorway as Heike tried to get me back on my feet or lying down on the ground.

Then, just as suddenly as it started, it stopped. I blinked a few times, wondering if it was about to return.

'Are you okay?' asked Heike, her voice a mixture of motherly care and professional concern.

I sat up, her hands helping to get my upper half vertical.

'I think so,' I managed to stammer. 'I don't know what that was,' I told her, knowing it was an inevitable next question for her to ask. 'I felt like I could see two different places at once.'

'Like two different realms?' Her question sent a chill through my core. She saw the look on my face. 'Do you think going there did something to you? Do you think Daniel has done something to you already?' I didn't know. I had no way of knowing. She gripped my right hand. 'Come on, let's get you on your feet and see if you can walk.'

We tried that and after a couple of minutes of assuring her that I was fine, she decided we had to get to the station. She pulled keys from her handbag. 'I'm driving. You are most definitely not.'

Chapter 6

At the station, I needed no escort this time because they had an ID to issue me. It was waiting at the front desk; Heike having called ahead to have it ready. The team were set up in the same room as before, but it was getting organised. More photographs had joined the previous ones and they were arranged on one wall now, grouped into clumps to show the two victims from Bremen. Above each was a time and date of the murder and the victim's name and photograph of the victim as he had been in life. To the right of them on the same wall, shown chronologically, were the other two identified victims: the uncle in the Czech Republic, a man in his fifties by the name of Jan Brychta, and a girl, this one from Schkeuditz, just outside Leipzig. Next to the uncle was another photograph with a line joining the two. It was of a young woman, probably a teenager still, her flawless skin and youthful looks convincing me that she was barely out of her childhood. I wondered where they would find her body. She was the niece of Jan Brychta, a young woman called Zuzana Brychta and she was listed as nineteen years old.

On another wall, there was a map of the northern half of Europe. The map was two metres high and three metres across, but I could see the pins sticking out of it. Two in Bremen, one almost on top of Brno in the Czech Republic and one close to Leipzig.

Muller wasn't present but as chief I figured he must have many tasks to divide his time. Nieswand was likewise absent but I learned he was attending a mandatory counselling session because of his recent kidnapping. I had to wonder if he would be lenient with the truth or just straight out tell the shrink he was being held by a demon and got rescued by a wizard and a werewolf. Moltz and Rugler were both using computers, pouring over research information no doubt and Voss was still off to one side, not exactly joining in but not exactly keeping out of it either.

'Where's Schenk?' asked Heike as she put her bag down on a handy desk.

The door twitched open again just as it was swinging shut. 'Right behind you,' he growled, coming in with a fresh machine dispensed coffee in his hands. He shot me a look. 'Have a nice lie in this morning?'

I didn't bother responding but then he wasn't waiting for me to, he was already across the room and talking to Moltz. 'Anything from the Czechs?'

Moltz pushed back from his computer terminal a little. 'I think we are going to have to go there if we want to know more. It's not that they are not forthcoming, but if we aren't going to tell them we think it's a werewolf, we will need to probe more closely ourselves.'

'Do that and I'll have you on report,' snapped Schenk. 'I'll not be made a laughing-stock in the police community.'

He swung his head around to see if I was going to say anything, but Heike got there first. 'Still in denial, Schenk?'

He stood up from his position leaning over the desk. 'Why do you think the chief has us locked up back here instead of in the pit with everyone else? They know we are working the Hoss murder from yesterday, but they have no idea the chief hired a wizard as some daft special liaison. When it gets out that we are suggesting a werewolf killed all these people, we will be a laughingstock, so you can be sure that I am approaching this from a sane angle. It's a man behind this. A totally nuts, clinically insane man, but a man, nonetheless. If you two want to help, you can go to the Czech Republic tomorrow. Brigitte in accounts will organise your travel.'

Heike squinted at him. 'Schenk, when they fully reinstate me later this week, you and I are going to have a conversation about rank which you will not enjoy.'

The tension in the room was keeping everyone else quiet, but I had no time nor desire for power games. In less than six days, I was going to go with Daniel to the immortal realm, so

I needed to sew this case up by then or forget about it. 'What contacts do we have in Brno? Are we meeting someone there?' I asked, crossing the room toward him and keeping my tone and volume normal to diffuse the situation.

Schenk looked down his nose at me. 'It's all on the screen.'

'Was the guy last night robbed as well?' I asked, looking at his pictures.

Moltz nodded. 'He was carrying the night's takings. It's his bar and he was attacked just a few metres from the back door. He only needed to cross the carpark to get to his car. He never made it.'

I looked at the pictures. He was better looking than the first man. Taller, clean-shaven and in his mid-thirties. He struck me as the sort of man who wouldn't have any trouble picking up girls. I moved to the information wall to see what I could learn there. Behind me, the door opened, the chief coming in looking harassed and sleep deprived as usual. His hair didn't look like he had brushed it in days, and he had crumbs in his beard.

Another man was hot on his heels. Once the door was shut, the chief introduced his companion, 'This is Eric Wengler, he is a profiler from Hamburg University. He contacted the commissioner and volunteered his services. So here he is.' The chief neither looked nor sounded happy about it and was doing very little to hide his opinion.

If Eric Wengler heard the chief's tone, he was happy to ignore it, the new man striding forward to start shaking hands with everyone. 'I shall try to remember names but please forgive me when I don't.' He was a short man, perhaps one metre sixty tall and lean like he had been on an extreme diet. I changed my mind as I observed him, decided instead that he looked more like an extreme runner; someone who might participate in double marathons and that sort of thing.

Everyone was introducing themselves by rank and name and briefly explaining what their role within the team was. When he got to me, I said, 'Otto Schneider, special consultant.'

He kept hold of my hand, looking up at me and frowning slightly. 'What field are you from?' he asked.

I knew what he was asking; he wanted to know why I was on the team if I wasn't a cop. He was there because he had a pertinent skill. To skip the whole thing forward, I said, 'I'm a wizard.'

Eric spluttered with laughter, but when no one else joined him, his eyes widened. He glanced about at the other team members and finally let my hand go. 'Right, yes, okay.' He tore his eyes from me so he could focus on the picture wall. 'Let's get stuck in then, shall we?'

An hour went by quickly, Nieswand returning after a while though he stayed tight-lipped about his encounter with the counsellor and no one brought the subject up. He was tasked with helping in the research element, which everyone in the room except Eric and I were focused on. Eric was making notes and asking occasional questions, interrupting the flow of research each time though I couldn't tell if he was going to prove useful at some point. I was the only one failing to add any value which was grating enough but Schenk's occasional glances of dismissal were really making me want to stick a flame up his butt.

There were no windows in our room, but I knew it when darkness fell and so did everyone else because I pretty much had a seizure.

Chapter 7

Falling to my knees with my hands gripping my skull got everyone's attention. They were all staring my way; Heike stood to see what was happening then asked me something. Just like before at my house, I could see her lips moving, but couldn't hear her; voices and other sounds were lost behind a wall of visual sensations as they bombarded my brain. This time though, I knew what I was seeing.

It was Katja Weber's house. The big place in Schwachhausen with the steps leading up to it and the owner who wanted to sue me for showing him what a small-minded idiot he was. I was seeing it with one eye again, my brain struggling to discern the images overlaying themselves inside my head. I would call it confusing, but such a simple word would miserably fail to capture how I felt.

There were hands on me, not that I could tell whose they were. It was a background distraction unable to make it through the images crowding my mind and suddenly, when a sense of anger and revenge flashed through me, I knew what I was seeing.

'It's Teague,' I managed through gritted teeth. I had to get up. I had to go. The demon I tried to kill was back for his familiar, reclaiming the prize I stole from him two nights ago. No one else was going to stop him; not that I was sure I could. Last time it had been a combined effort between Zachary and me that had beaten him, but he wasn't really beaten, just incapacitated for a while after I exploded every cell in his body from the inside. You might expect that to kill a person, to kill anything anywhere in the universe, but the demons had some crazy magic going on that made them immortal. I wasn't up to speed on how it worked, but regardless of any of it, a fifteen-year-old girl needed my help and I was going to answer the call.

Snarling as I forced the image from my head, I got the knuckles of my right fist onto the carpet tiles and pushed myself off the floor. Heike's concerned face was right in front of mine. 'You think Teague is here?'

'Who's Teague,' asked Schenk.

I didn't hang around to answer anyone's questions, instead I was heading for the door, staggering like I had been drinking again, but I knew where I needed to go and there was no time to waste. At the door, I remembered that I didn't have a car. 'I need a lift,' I blurted, reaching for Heike unnecessarily as she was already following me.

'Hey!' yelled Schenk. 'Where do you think you're going? We have an ongoing investigation.'

I didn't stop my forward movement, but I did spin on my heels, shifting my feet to walk backwards and giving him the bird. I wanted to tell him a girl was about to be kidnapped by a demon and dragged to a life of slavery in an alternate realm, but doing so would cause him to follow me, or send others to follow me, and that would endanger them. I didn't want Heike with me either, but I could try to lose her when we got close to the house.

By the time we hit the pit, where half the cops in the station were working, we were running, Heike understanding the urgency I felt. Schenk sent Moltz and Nieswand to follow us, the pair of them bursting through the door behind us just before we reached the pit's far side.

Heike didn't need me to prompt her to drive fast, she was already risking our lives and others by driving faster than the conditions would allow. The roads were clear of snow, of course, the municipal services geared up and well-practiced in dealing with freezing temperatures, but the grit that kept the ice from reforming didn't get everywhere and cars coming in from other areas brought snow with them that fell from beneath their wheel arches and off their roofs.

'What are you doing there?' she asked, twitching her eyes across my side of the car to see what I was fiddling with. I had taken a small Tupperware box from my pocket and was now fiddling with its contents.

'These are protection rings,' I told her.

'They look a bit small,' she frowned. 'And a bit feminine.'

'That's because they are a woman's rings. I need to buy some that fit me, but I haven't had time to do that since we got back from the other side.' In truth, I could have made time, but I had forgotten the need.

'And the tape?'

'They're a woman's rings; they don't fit past my first knuckles, so I have to stick them to my fingers.'

'Riiiight,' she drawled just as she hit a turning and damned near had the car on two wheels to get it around. I swore as my life flashed before my eyes. 'Everything okay?' asked Heike, her voice calm.

'Yes, why?'

'Because your knuckles have gone white and you looked terrified.' She made the observation as she power-slid her soccer mum car through a red light, slammed the gear stick down two gears and mashed the accelerator.

'Let's just say I'm not worried about fighting Teague anymore.'

She smiled sweetly at me. 'Why's that?' she asked, inviting me to walk over the trapdoor.

I knew it was there, but I went for it anyway. 'Because I don't expect to live long enough to face him.'

She cut her eyes at me and looked ready to snap a retort in my direction when a blast of horn brought her attention back to the road. She said several un-lady-like words as the car twitched and slid, opposing forces, rather than lack of friction, nearly sending it into a parked car.

Despite my concerns, we slid to a stop outside the Weber's property a few minutes later, Heike taking me all the way there because I forgot to get her to stop short. The front door was already open, light spilling from it as if trying to escape the horror inside.

I shouted, 'Wait here,' as I ran up the driveway.

'Like hell I will,' she shouted, Heike chasing after me whether I wanted her to or not.

'There's nothing you can do here, Heike,' I argued, predicting that I was wasting my time no matter what argument I presented. 'You don't even have your gun back.'

She didn't argue. She didn't stop either, so as I got to the steps, I hit her with a blast from an air spell to send her tumbling and dashed inside. She would take offense and probably make me pay later, but it was for her own good. I, at least, had barrier spells and the ability to wield elemental magic that would give me a fighting chance.

I slammed the door shut as I went through it, for all the good that would do, and paused in the Webers' threshold. Panting slightly and berating myself for letting my fitness slide, I drew in a deep breath. 'Teague!' I bellowed.

There was silence in the house, but it was a sudden silence, like you get when everyone is listening and holding their breath. Then a woman screamed, Frau Weber I thought, not Katja, but it was cut off as quickly as it started and followed by a thump that sounded just like a person's body hitting the carpet.

My feet were moving before I told them to, driving me along the hallway to the foot of the stairs which is where I found the start of the destruction. The stairs had wooden spokes running up the sides but many of them were broken, smashed to smithereens in a way that made them look like they had been exploded from within. There were scorch marks in places on the walls and a general smell of burning in the air.

I took the stairs two or three at a time, holding a defensive spell in front of me and bouncing off the wall with a shoulder where the mid-point landing performed a U-turn. I kept my arms up and a spell ready, but I didn't have to search for Teague, he was waiting for me. Dressed in trousers, shirt, and a waistcoat, the retirement age looking demon looked elegant but deranged nevertheless, his insane eyes and crooked smile letting me know there was no chance to reason with him.

'Wizard,' he sneered looking at me with an expression that suggested my arrival was a dream come true. Then he giggled, a small but worrying sound that had no place in our current environment. He had more to say, 'A foolish mortal wielding insignificant elemental magic.' He was aiming for arrogant superiority and getting pretty close. It was hard to focus on his face though because he had Katja hanging from his right hand. He had a fistful of her top and had dragged her onto the upper landing to meet me. Behind them, I could see Frau Weber barely conscious on the floor of Katja's room. She was moving about and trying to get up but seemed groggy and disorientated.

Katja was fighting still but she was a gnat flailing against a dog, a nuisance perhaps, but Teague could kill her in a flash.

My ability to fight was hampered. Katja was a human shield protecting Teague from most of the spells I would want to unleash. When last we fought, we were in his house and I hit him with everything I could conjure, no concern at all for fires I might light or damage I might do. It was different here, but the cogent part of my brain assured me it was better to blow the roof off the Webers' house than to let the demon take their daughter.

Yet again I didn't have the swords I picked out for fights just like this. The cops wouldn't let me carry them, not that I asked, and they said no; I figured it was a given. So here I was, facing a demon who had an arsenal many times more powerful than mine and I couldn't even use my best spells on him for fear of harming the very girl I came here to protect.

All that played through my head as I mounted the last couple of steps and reached the landing. Teague wasted no time in trying to kill me, launching a bolt of red death from his left hand. It hit my defensive barrier, burning out the spell that made it instantly. I whispered the word to activate the next ring, my protective barrier only down for a bare fraction of a second. Then I pushed an air spell against him.

I was trying too hard to avoid Katja, so the spell had no impact at all, ruffling his hair as it wafted by. This was no good, I was an open target, a second ball of hell fire from his left hand knocking down another of my barrier spells.

Eight remaining. It wouldn't take long to exhaust them all, so I tried something new, something I last tried on the human wizard, Edward Blake, in the morgue. I ran at Teague and swung a punch at his face.

I had to duck a third blast of hellfire as I closed the distance between us, but he wasn't forming them as fast as I thought he could, or perhaps as fast as he ought to be able to. He was distracted by Katja I knew, and by Frau Weber who was back on her feet and looking for a hard object to use as a weapon. Either way, his shot went over my head as I spun around and down to avoid it, dropping my defensive spell at the last moment so it wouldn't act as a battering ram against him, and, more importantly, Katja.

His eyes went wide in surprise as he saw my fist flying upward, but he didn't react in any way that was going to save him from the blow. It connected under his chin, slamming his head back until muscle and bone stopped it from going any further. At that point, the energy in my punch hadn't dissipated, so the rest of his body followed his head, pulling him over backwards and causing him to drop Katja.

She tumbled to the carpet, bouncing painfully and gasping, but rolling to get clear so I knew she was lucid. What I hadn't counted on was Teague automatically summoning hell fire as he fell.

The shots flew wild from both hands, unaimed as they were, one striking the ceiling and going through it, another hitting a painting and blasting it from the wall. I threw myself at him before he could recover. I wanted to pummel him, using my fists and feet and anything else I could bring to the party in a bid to knock him out, but I wasn't sure I could achieve such a feat and I needed to get his hands under control: he couldn't kill me or anyone else if he couldn't use his weapons.

Landing with a leading elbow to his gut, I heard the air rush from his lungs, but it didn't stop the next two shots from flying, adding to the smell of burning already in the air as smouldering from previous shots became small fires. The fact that small fires wouldn't stay small compounding my problems.

I had hold of his fists, trying to keep them closed while I wondered what the hell I could do next. He was too powerful to be allowed to live and far too immortal for me to kill. I couldn't use my hands either though so there were no spells being conjured and a stalemate of sorts had been reached.

Teague knew it too, glaring at me with his head lifted off the carpet. 'I'm going to torture you so slowly, you'll think it's a career, wizard.' His eyes were crazy, and as I looked into them, I saw red sparks zipping about inside the irises. 'You took my slave, wizard.'

'You mean the girl?' I managed from between gritted teeth.

'Yes,' he hissed. 'She was my familiar. Finally, after four thousand years I had a familiar again and in less than a day you took her from me. I will have her back and I will have my revenge. You humiliated me. Just as I was gaining status, you humiliated me!' he screamed the final words, rage filling them as he fought to break free.

Fear gripped me because I knew I couldn't hold him. Not indefinitely. He looked like an old man, late sixties or something like that, but he was strong, and he was deadly, and most scarily of all, I was worried that he might just be insane. He grinned at me, and I saw how poorly prepared I was. A second later, he hit me with one of my own weapons: lightning. Elemental magic conjured by his hands. Not his most powerful tool perhaps, but effective, nevertheless.

All he did was lift a single finger and point it at me, sucking in all the moisture from the air to create lightning from the friction within the cells. The blast hit me in the shoulder and not my face only because I sensed it was coming and threw myself backward at the last moment. What it hit didn't make much difference to the overall effect though, I was lifted from my feet and hurled backwards, my back and shoulder striking the wall painfully.

I was about to die. I felt certain of that because I knew how long it would take Teague to summon two orbs of hell fire and it wasn't very long at all. Less time than it was going to take me to summon my next barrier, that was for certain.

So, it was with some degree of surprise that I had time to bounce off the wall and slump all the way to the floor. My eyes had closed from the pain, an involuntary reaction as my consciousness swam and came back under my control. As they reopened, I discovered why I was still alive: Katja was standing in Teague's way.

And she was trying to conjure a spell.

One of the people I rescued from the immortal realm said she was the most promising of those Daniel had taken, in his opinion. That was why he gave her to Teague. Quite what Daniel got from it, I didn't know. Maybe I would find out about that soon enough, but right now, the only thing that interested me was turning Teague inside out if I could.

I would be damned if I was going to let him take Katja again.

Katja had watched me, that was obvious in her movements. She was unrefined, untrained, much as I had been two decades ago, but what she was doing reflected what she had seen me do and she had a natural sense of what was the right thing. What she was doing or trying to do wasn't important right now though. Her movements distracted the demon for the half second I needed to conjure my own spell: that was the important bit.

I ripped it from my right hand using my left to control it and pushed it into Teague just like I had the last time we met. Maybe this time it would stick. Deep down I suspected elemental magic was supposed to be used for positive activities, somehow making the world better each time it was employed. If that was the case, then there might be some kind of planetary rebalancing coming my way because I used it almost exclusively for pain and death.

Right now was no exception.

My spell gripped the water inside his body, and I pushed heat into his cells knowing I needed only a few seconds to explode him from the inside. I had done it before. It was deeply unpleasant, but it worked.

Teague's hands were raised to blast me and Katja with fresh bolts of hell fire, but they faltered now as my spell gripped his central nervous system. He would die. Unfortunately, he would then come back because he was annoyingly immortal. I did it anyway, pushing more and more ley line energy into his atoms, but as I neared the brink from which he would explode and then somehow return, he began to fight back.

A look of concentration formed a mask on his face as I stepped in front of Katja. I was forming a protective barrier for her now, but my left hand lingered on her shoulder, attempting to impart strength and courage as he began to push my spell away.

Maybe it was because I had done this before, and he knew he could survive it. Maybe it was simply that I caught him by surprise last time, but he was stronger than me and both of us knew it. Whatever the case was, he was pushing my spell down, lowering the heat I pushed into his cells even as I tried harder to force heat into them.

Behind me, I could both hear and feel Katja trying hard to summon her own magic. Whether she could produce anything helpful wasn't a factor I had considered; she was young and untrained and for all I knew, had never cast a spell in her life. I got ready to switch spells; this one wasn't working anyway. Then, from the corner of my eye, I saw Frau Weber cowering just inside the door of Katja's bedroom and saw an opportunity.

I dropped the lightning spell I had planned to use and switched to using air, creating a wall of it to push Teague backwards a metre. His feet slid over the carpet as it caught him unawares. 'Go!' I screamed at Frau Weber. She hesitated, necessitating a jerk of my head. 'Get Katja and run!'

Frozen to the spot in terror, she couldn't get her feet to move. Katja, on the other hand, was already moving, snagging her mother's arm to yank her forward. They could escape behind me to reach the stairs and get out of the house.

A new voice came from behind me, 'Quickly!' It was Heike, inside the house but wise enough to hold back. She would still kick my ass when this was over. If I survived, that is.

Feet thundered down the stairs which felt like permission to unleash anything and everything I could find in my arsenal. So, I did, knocking him back with another air spell and forming lightning as he stumbled. He blasted me with two fresh bolts of hellfire, destroying another barrier. It hadn't taken him long to learn to keep his distance, effectively preventing me from engaging him physically again. I really needed to get him outside, it just wasn't safe to use fire and lightning indoors and my most powerful of spells, earth, wasn't possible until we were standing on it. Fortune played into my hands for once though as I threw the lightning, missed him and blew out a chunk of wall.

Herr Weber was going to take exception to that, not that I cared because I suddenly had what I wanted: a way to get Teague out of the house. Beginning to feel tired from the effort, I gritted my teeth and threw maximum effort into my next air spell, forming a wall of air and making it spin like a tornado. It snatched paintings from the walls and blew doors open along the corridor, but with no wall to trap it, the air flowed along and out, carrying a jumbled, tumbling version of Teague with it.

I followed him to the ragged hole in the wall, running along the corridor as I dropped the spell. Skidding to a halt where the wall used to be, I got to watch Teague hit the snow-covered grass outside. He was an ungraceful lump by this point, but he was far from done. Even as I watched, what should have been his broken body bounced, rolled over, and came to rest facing down. Only for a second though; as I looked, he was already beginning to get up. He was on the opposite side of the house to the front door where I would exit if I ran down the stairs to get out, so I tried something I have never even attempted before.

I tried to fly.

It's one of those things that you wonder about while lying awake in bed at night or soaking in the bath. I can create a wall of air, so if I aim that downwards would I be able to fly? I had seen Edward Blake do exactly that, so I knew it was possible and thought I knew how to do it. Flying, in fact, wasn't really the aim, gliding a distance over the ground would do and that was what I tried right now, stepping out of the window and pushing against the earth to stop myself from falling.

It sort of worked.

I fell, caught myself, fell some more and caught myself again and finally landed in a mess on some snow that turned out to have a shrub underneath it. A spiky, spiteful shrub at that.

No one was around to see me, which, given the exploding wall and the noise from battling Teague, seemed surprising. I was at the back of the house and Teague was right in front of me, back on his feet and turning to face me as he formed two fresh balls of hell fire.

'You are strong, wizard. Maybe I will take you as my familiar instead. Not as visually appealing but already able to do so much more than the girl.' Did this mean he was going to stop trying to kill me? Two blasts of hellfire which destroyed the next barrier I held for my protection told me that was not the case, but a voice from my left stopped us both before the next volleys could be launched.

'He is already spoken for.' The sound of the familiar voice spun me around. Daniel was here. He had Katja and Frau Weber with him, each of them held firmly around the back of their delicate necks as he pushed them forward. He wasn't alone though; he had another pair of demons with him and a gang of about twenty shilt. The shilt were wearing enchantments to disguise their features, their reptilian faces and triangular teeth visible only to me with my second sight. The other demons were a man and a woman, both older than Daniel appeared to be and far less attractive. The woman was lean, bordering on skinny and the man was taller and quite overweight, a large belly hanging over his trousers at the front. They both had twin orbs of hellfire ready to throw and were shepherding Heike and officers Nieswand and Moltz. Were they here to collect me?

'I have five days,' I protested.

Daniel cocked an eyebrow at me. 'Indeed, Otto. I am not here for you. I am here to collect my errant colleague.'

Teague snarled in response, 'I want my prize. The prize you promised me.'

'And you shall have a prize. It will not be this one though, my friend. We discussed this, did we not?'

'I did not agree,' Teague snapped back.

Daniel sighed. 'Your agreement is not necessary. I bargained with this wizard and agreed to the return of the girl in exchange for his passage to the mortal realm. I promised you a superior replacement.'

'I don't want a replacement. I want vengeance. The wizard came into my home and attacked me.'

'Yes, he did,' snapped Daniel, showing irritation for the first time. 'Successfully. A human besting one of us is something that hasn't happened in thousands of years. So long ago, in fact, that it last happened when we were mortal, and they could creep up on us with a spear. I granted him the girl's freedom and you will honour that.'

Teague twitched again. Daniel saw it, his eye scrutinising the elder demon. He also saw Teague reach a decision: he was going to try to kill me again and perhaps everyone else.

Daniel fired first, his blast of hellfire taking Teague off his feet. It was quickly followed by another and another as the two demons with Daniel joined in. Teague was down and he was groaning as smoke rose from his body.

Still squinting at the fallen demon, Daniel started walking in my direction. Behind him the shilt were holding the humans but were not attempting to prey on them. Heike, Katja, and the others all looked terrified and rightly wanted to escape but they were held tight and without weapons.

I lowered my arms, unwilling to start a fresh fight against such terrible odds. Maybe I would be able to hold them off for a while, but I doubted I could stop them from doing whatever it was they were here to do. Wearily I faced Daniel as he closed the distance to me, but what he said came as a big surprise.

'I'm sorry, Otto. I should have known he would try something like this. So many of those who once held senior positions are unable to let their power go, even so long after the death curse trapped us.'

My head filled with questions again; there was so much I didn't know or understand. I went with the one I needed to know the answer to, 'Why are you here?'

Daniel looked surprised as if the answer was obvious. 'To stop him from breaking my word. He has not fully recovered from what you did to him. He is immortal, stuck that way due to some very powerful magic, but you broke him down into atoms and though he recovered quickly enough physically, he… isn't quite himself.'

'You're not here to take me away?'

'Goodness no, Otto. You have five days still as promised.'

'And you're not going to take the girl?'

'Katja? No. Again, I gave you my word and what are we without our integrity?' he paused and was clearly waiting for me to fill in the answer to his question. When I didn't, he deflated somewhat, his big punchline spoiled. 'Human, Otto. We would be human without our integrity. Your race steals and squabbles and lies and cheats at every opportunity. It's a wonder you haven't wiped each other out.' All I could do was stare at him. Silence stretched on for a beat until Daniel clapped his hands together and motioned for his companions. Teague was just starting to get up again. 'Let's collect our friend and be going, shall we?'

'Really? That's it?' I asked.

As he formed a shimmering portal of air, Daniel watched the shilt help Teague into it then turned to me. 'Five days, Otto. Use them wisely.'

'Wait,' I called after him. When he paused, I said, 'There's something I have to know.'

'All in good time,' he replied and started to move again.

'What did you do to my wife?' I yelled before he could step through the portal and vanish. It wasn't the first time I had asked him that question. Two nights ago, after the battle at Teague's house, I demanded he tell me, but he refused; holding all the cards, he said he would tell me later. This was later.

Again, he paused. He was half in and half out of the portal now, but he turned his head to look at me. 'I came for you, Otto. I could sense magic at your house. It was obvious someone had been pulling ley line energy so I came to find that person knowing they would make a good familiar if I could train them. I thought the person I wanted was your wife. Or maybe that should be hoped it was. Everyone seems to want female familiars; they're more docile.'

'What did you do to her?' I demanded through clenched teeth, my anger and frustration boiling.

'Do, Otto? I didn't do anything. Your poor wife panicked when I appeared. She slipped and fell. It happened right before you came in. Did she die?' He asked the question so matter of factly that I wanted to kill him.

'No,' I growled.

'Pity,' he replied. 'Now she will have to miss you.'

Then he was gone, the portal closing with a faint popping noise to leave me staring at nothing. Gathering myself, though I felt like crap, I went to see who among the humans was hurt.

From the shadows by the house, Special Investigator Voss stepped out to make himself visible. We locked eyes for a second. 'I need to report this,' he announced as he pulled a phone from a pocket, the light from the screen illuminating his face as he made a call.

Ignoring him, I focused my attention on the fifteen-year-old girl who had almost been kidnapped for the second time in less than a week. She looked scared but was holding it together in contrast to her mother. Frau Weber was a hysterical mess. Rather than the daughter clinging to the mother for security, I was witnessing it the other way around. Officer Nieswand looked thrown by the encounter with the demons too; rigidly quiet and staring at nothing as if trapped inside the moment still and Moltz was looking at me with new-found respect. He was yet another officer to witness magic and supernatural beings first-hand. He was taking it quite well.

'Are you hurt?' I asked Heike, touching her arm as she tried to assist the Webers.

'No,' she replied. 'No, I'm fine. I didn't resist and I made sure Moltz and Nieswand surrendered too. They arrived just as we got back outside. They would have been here sooner, but they got stuck behind a crash; the ice causing havoc again.'

The sound of distant sirens got our attention.

'We should move around to the front of the house,' murmured Moltz. Then, looking up at the hole in the back wall of the Webers' beautiful house, he asked, 'Did the house catch on fire?'

Oh, nuts.

Chapter 8

The Webers' place had indeed been on fire, but it was minor, not the house-gutting kind of fire it might have been if Moltz hadn't brought my attention to it. As the police officers escorted Frau Weber and Katja around to the front of the house, I briefly considered showing off by flying back up to the hole I created. I dismissed the notion as foolhardy though; given how poorly and beaten I felt and that I had only done it once, I was as likely to slam into the building or shoot straight over it to land on my head in the street the other side. Plus, I wasn't sure how many more reality challenging events Moltz could witness tonight without him folding into a gibbering mess.

So, I jogged/slid around to the front of the house and ran in through the front door. An older couple across the street called out to ask if everything was alright, but I left Heike to deal with them as I dashed inside and up the stairs.

Putting fires out is easy enough if you can magically command the water vapour in the air to coalesce into droplets. There were no electrical wires or anything else near the small flames licking up the wall in several spots where the hellfire had struck, so they went out easily enough. Their house was trashed though. Looking around, I felt bad. Not that I would do it differently next time, but I could see sky through a hole in the roof, there was a very obvious hole in the rear façade of the house, and the upper landing would need a lot of paint, carpet, and other work. I figured they could afford it though I was curious to learn what they would write as the cause on their insurance forms.

I found the group outside in the snow. More police were arriving as I came out of the house but there were already three cars parked haphazardly on the drive with the cops trying to work out what they were supposed to do now. Moltz and Nieswand were dealing with them while Heike had Frau Weber and Katja off to one side.

The Webers looked cold, understandably, since they hadn't dressed to be outside. They hadn't been wearing shoes when we were inside, but they were now, Heike, or someone, snagging some from the downstairs lobby along with the coats they now wore.

I wanted to speak with Katja before I left or lost the chance. I also wanted to visit Kerstin in the hospital and felt an almost overwhelming need to lie down – conjuring multiple spells one after the other always leaves me feeling spent plus my winter cold was kicking the crap out of me. Talking to the young girl proved easier than expected though because she was looking to speak with me. As I came down the steps from their house, she caught my eye and moved away from her mother, a whispered something and a hug kept her mother in place.

We met halfway across the drive, the girl clearly very cold as she hugged herself and shivered inside her coat. I steered her toward a squad car. 'Can we warm up in the back?' I asked a cop loitering by the driver's door and indicated the teenage girl. I got a single nod in response as he talked on his radio. The car was pleasantly warm, the blast of heat from it instantly welcome as Katja slid in and then along the back seat to make room for me. We were alone in the car and no one else could hear us.

'Am I a witch?' she asked without prompting.

I guess the question had been going around in her head for a while with no opportunity for it to be posed. Making eye contact with her, I said, 'I'm not qualified to answer that question I'm afraid. I don't really know what I am either.' As soon as I said the words, I realised I had taken the wrong approach. Katja was looking for answers and expected me to have them. I might not have them all, but the right approach would be to put a helpful spin on what I did know. As disappointment gripped her features, I said, 'What I mean is; the demons refer to me as a wizard, but I don't know if the name matters. I have been able to wield the elements since I was about fourteen. I have learned a lot in the twenty years since my abilities manifested and call myself a wizard because I don't know what other term to use. I am able to control air and water and earth. Through that ability I can create lightning and conjure fire and I have taught myself a few other skills such as the ability to track a person and to be able to hear when a person is lying to me. Have you experimented much to see what you can do?'

Katja's pose betrayed her discomfort at discussing the subject. She was fiddling her hands around nervously and looking anywhere but at my face. I gave her time; I could tell she was working up to say something. 'I didn't know what it was. I kept getting dreams; really vivid ones, and in the dreams, I was able to do magic. Not like you see on the television where they do stuff with cards, but like what you describe, like the things I just saw you do with air and lightning, but I didn't know how to make it happen once I was awake.' She fell silent again, her mouth twitching as she tried to form the next sentence. 'Then, a few months ago... there's a girl at school who was mean to me. She's always mean to me because my dad has money and hers doesn't. It seems funny that it works that way: on television it's always the rich girl who is the bitch.' Katja kept pausing in her retelling. I waited each time for her to restart. 'She cornered me, her and her awful friends, Nina and Franka. I thought she was going to hit me and when I raised my hand to ward her off, somehow I made a pulse of air. It was like you were doing upstairs to push Teague back but not as strong. Anyway, it knocked them over and that scared them; they haven't bothered me since, but I knew for certain then that I wasn't normal. That's why Daniel came for me, isn't it?'

I nodded my head. 'Yes, I think so.'

Her quiet voice asked, 'Do you know other people like us?'

This time I shook my head. 'No. The first time I ever met anyone else that could wield magic like me was last week. You are only the second, but I believe there may be many more like us.'

'But I'm not like you,' she protested. 'I can't do what you can do; produce fire or lightning or track people.'

I placed a hand gently on top of hers. 'You can't do those things *yet*.' I put real emphasis on the last word. 'I couldn't either at fifteen. I had no one to teach me so I had to work it out for myself.'

Her eyes were wide with hope now. 'Are you going to be my teacher?' Her question caught me by surprise. Inadvertently, I just volunteered for the job when I said I hadn't had a teacher, but the idea of taking her on had never crossed my mind. It sort of terrified me too; I wasn't any good with children. She was nearly a woman at fifteen, she certainly looked like one despite the youth in her face, but I doubted anyone would approve of me spending alone time with an attractive fifteen-year-old girl. Especially not if I ever referred to her out loud as attractive.

Stuttering, I found an excuse and clung to it. 'I only have five days. I promised to go with Daniel, if you remember. That was the price of bringing us home.' She looked utterly crestfallen, a tear forming in the corner of her right eye. It nudged me to act. I held up my right hand. 'Copy me,' I instructed.

She mimicked my motion.

Then, as I watched her hands, I concentrated on what I was doing and tried my hardest to explain it, 'I can feel the energy of the Earth as it moves through ley lines. Our magic comes from them because we have the ability to draw on it.' I dropped my second sight into place and looked down. A fine tendril of line energy was flowing up through the car and into Katja. 'Can you see the energy?'

She gave me a confused look.

'I call it my second sight.' I was about to explain how I brought my second sight into play, but it wasn't something I had ever considered before. I could remember the first time it happened for me, but I was going to have to think hard about how to help her do it. I was struggling for words. 'I feel it inside my head, a sense of the magic, or the power of the earth itself. For me it helps if I close my eyes. I do that and then feel the energy. I can see the ley lines with my eyes closed and when I open them, it's like an overlay or an additional filter.'

'Like looking though an infrared camera?' Katja asked. 'Like you can see the people but now you are seeing their heat instead?'

I considered her analogy. 'Kind of, yes. I see a golden hue when I look at supernatural creatures. I can see one around you now. I think it is your aura.'

'I'm supernatural,' she murmured as an excited whisper, clearly delighted by the concept.

'Can you see the energy?' I asked again.

She nodded, staring around and about and then at me. 'You have an aura too,' she breathed.

'Now gently pull energy into your right hand. Focus it there and reach out with it, sensing the air around you, touching it with your magic. We are going to perform an air spell, just a small one. It will be something to practice. Focus on getting one thing right until you can do it without having to think and then move on to a different skill. Ready?'

'Yes.' Her voice came out as an excited squeak.

'Use your left hand to control the spell. Use it to form the air and push it away from yourself. On the count of three, let it go and try to make the air freshener on the rear-view mirror move.' She glanced at the target and back at her hands, biting her top lip as she concentrated. 'One.' I watched her, sensing the energy in her hands and knowing she had exactly what I had. If I could, I would teach her; imbue her with the ability to defend herself maybe. 'Two.' She had raw ability. How different might my life have been if there had been someone to teach me twenty years ago. 'Three.'

All the windows in the car exploded outwards instantaneously.

Katja squealed in shock and I said a very bad word. Every pair of eyes was staring our way.

'What the hell just happened?' asked the cop standing by the driver's door still. He had bent down to look inside, his face filled with question and his eyes as wide as dinner plates.

'I think there might be something wrong with the car.' I suggested. 'Might need a factory recall.' Then, softly to Katja, I said, 'I think we should get out.'

Frau Weber and Heike were right outside as we exited the car. 'Everything okay, Otto?' asked Heike with a single raised eyebrow.

'Um, yes,' I replied, wondering whether she would demand a more detailed explanation. The driver was coming my way, his face unable to decide whether it was confused about how it had happened or angry about the amount of paperwork this would cause.

I got a finger thrust toward me as he advanced. 'You're that stinking fake Schenk is telling everyone about.'

Heike swung in front to block him from getting to me. 'Stand down, Mattiske. I won't tell you again.' Her voice was calm, even, and utterly certain of obedience on his part. If he wanted to retort, he didn't get the chance because a radio message hit all the cops at once. Something resembling a huge wolf had just been spotted near the docks and it was walking on its back legs.

Chapter 9

The cop with all the blown-out windows got left behind to wait for a recovery vehicle and to guard the scene at the Webers' as most of the other cops dived into cars and hauled butt. Heike was going for her car and I ran after her, fearing that the cops might shoot first and ask questions very much later. If it was Zachary we were all chasing, I wanted to get to him first.

Katja grabbed my arm as I started to move away. 'Take me with you,' she begged.

I was lost for words. 'I can't,' I started to say, and, of course, I couldn't, but that wouldn't work as an argument. So, I said, 'Your mother needs you,' turning the sentence around in my head so I didn't tell her to stay with her mum like a child and made her feel like the brave one instead. I had to go, but as I backed away, I said, 'We'll speak again soon.'

'Come on, wizard!' shouted Heike, already in her car and shouting through the open passenger window. She even started moving before I got to the car, forcing me to match pace by running alongside and jumping in.

'Is that in the police safety handbook?' I asked flippantly. 'And what's with everyone calling me wizard suddenly. Telling the whole world about me is not a good idea.'

Heike just snorted a little chuckle and swung the car into the street, bouncing off the kerb as the rear end slid around in the snow. There was a police radio in her car, and it was in constant chatter, messages back and forth from excited people in the dispatch room and cops already on the ground at the docks. The roads were so empty it would only take us ten minutes to get there, but by then whatever was going to happen would be over.

Frustratingly, I was right.

Heike stayed on the tail of the police car in front, driving her soccer mum car expertly through the snowy conditions despite its comparative lack of power and handling. We arrived at Bremen harbour to find a gaggle of cars and cops standing around doing not very much at all. Mostly they were leaning on their open car doors and talking about what had occurred.

'It went over the wall,' one claimed, achieving centre stage because, in his words, he and his female partner had damned near run into it. The sighting was reported by a dockworker, a man in a high crane whose job was to empty cargo vessels at the dock. He reported a large mammal walking upright and even had a fuzzy picture on his phone which every news channel would show later that evening. He wasn't the only one who had seen it and the two recent murders were all over the news already, their grizzly nature guaranteeing them top billing.

No one had been hurt this time, but the multiple reports of a large, bipedal, wolf-like creature drew the police, who arrived at both ends of the dock by luck rather than coordination. One set of officers flushed the creature towards the others, but it escaped over an impossibly high wall and into a shipping container park where they lost it.

I listened in silence, adding nothing and giving no opinion though I noted the word werewolf came up more than once in the discussions around me. From their description and the faint photograph they had from the man's phone, I had to admit that it sounded like the way I would describe Zachary: tall, broad shouldered, powerful looking with a wolf's head and long claws.

Whether it was him or whether it was not, we had missed him and there was no longer any reason to hang about.

'I'm heading home,' Heike told me, nudging my arm to get my attention. 'Can I drop you back at your house?'

'Can you drop me at the hospital, please?'

'You really feel that bad? You sure don't look well.' I thought for a moment she was going to check my forehead with her hand like she would one of her children. If she thought of doing so, she managed to change her mind before muscle memory lifted her arm.

I did feel bad; sick and shaky and weak and just full of bone-deep aches. I kept telling myself it was just a bad case of the snuffles, but I wasn't entirely convinced. That wasn't why I wanted to go to the hospital though. 'My wife,' I said simply.

She nodded in understanding and we travelled in silence until a phone call from Detective Sergeant Schenk made us both jump.

'Dressler,' Heike said to answer the call.

It came through on the car's hands-free system, so I heard it when he asked, 'Where are you?'

Heike blew out a short breath of annoyance that she had to answer to the fool until she was reinstated. 'We responded to the report of a wolf-like creature at the docks. It was all over before we got there. Now I'm heading home and I'm going to drop Otto at the hospital to see his wife.'

'You need to come back to the station,' he barked in reply. 'Your travel tickets are here. Your flight is at 0600hrs tomorrow.'

Heike swore quietly. Then turned to me with an angry face. 'He knows I have children. Just wait until I get my badge back,' she hissed. Then at normal volume she said, 'I'll report in tomorrow when we land and let you know how it goes. The team can email me with any new findings overnight.'

'I want you straight back here afterward. There's a flight back at four o'clock. Be on it and come straight to the station for debriefing.'

I saw her muttering about where she was going to shove her badge. 'Anything else?' she asked.

'Not yet. Be ready for changes.' Then he hung up. He really was an arse. It was possible that he considered this murder case to be high profile enough to aid his career and was just trying to be effective and efficient. I suspected though that he had been given too much power to wield and was using it primarily to even up some imaginary scorecard.

'He thinks Brno is a wild-goose chase, you know,' Heike remarked. 'That's why he is sending us. He wants you out of the way and he doesn't want me there to tell him what he is getting wrong. He figures he can have a day without either one of us. If they manage to somehow solve the case or catch the killer before we return, he can claim it was all him. He'll probably claim we were goofing off in the Czech Republic.'

I couldn't argue with her thoughts, but there was nothing I could do about it and nothing Heike could do until her hearing process was complete. Failing to be a good girl until then would not go in her favour, so we were stuck with Detective Sergeant Schenk and his determined need to be a dickhead.

None of us knew how wrong we all were about the Czech Republic.

Chapter 10

At the reception desk to my wife's ward I met Nurse Christiana Makatsch. I made a point of learning names when it first became obvious my wife was not going to recover quickly. I was here every day and there weren't that many faces to memorise, but she took one look at me and rushed out from behind the desk where she was sorting through cardboard files.

'Herr Schneider are you sick?' she asked, her worried expression telling me I must look even worse than I felt.

'I'm something,' I replied feeling worse now that she had drawn attention to my ailments.

Now it was her turn to grab my arm, using both her hands to steer me toward a chair. 'Let's get you sat down and give you a quick check over.'

'Is that necessary?' I asked. I knew she was doing her job and trying to look after me, but I had a winter cold and no medicine in the world could fix it. I resigned myself to that fact last night; I just needed to tough it out until it passed.

Feeling my pulse and checking her watch, the answer I got was, 'The patients here almost all have a lowered immune system. If you are ill, I will not be able to let you see your wife, Herr Schneider.'

Irrational anger welled up and I had to fight to control my voice so I wouldn't snap. I only had five days left to see my wife and didn't know how often I would be able to return after I went with Daniel. Maybe I wouldn't get to return at all. More and more I wanted to regret agreeing to his terms, but I hadn't had a choice at the time and I still didn't have one now. 'I really need to see her,' I said as calmly as I could.

As if brushing my statement aside, she said, 'Your pulse is very fast. Do you feel hot?'

I sighed. I couldn't berate or argue with her. 'Yes,' I admitted. Then, because I knew she would have a stack of follow on questions, I listed all my symptoms and told her when they started. Fifteen minutes later I was still sitting in the chair but now there was a doctor examining me, a young man whose age suggested he had to be fresh out of med school. My temperature was elevated, but within tolerable levels, my pulse was fast but not dangerously so, but he disagreed with my diagnosis of winter cold or influenza.

'I'm going to take a blood sample, Herr Schneider. We can rule a lot of things out with that and the results will be back within the hour.' Resigning myself to it, since they were not going to let me see Kerstin until they knew what I had, I rolled up my sleeve and pumped my fist a few times to raise a vein.

'Nice accessible veins.' He was talking to himself more than to me but accessible or not, it still took him two attempts to get the needle into one. He took three vials before drawing the needle out again, stepping out of the way as Nurse Makatsch moved in ready with a blob of cotton wool and a strip of sticky gauze.

'I'll come back as soon as I have the results, Herr Schneider,' the young doctor told me on his way to the door. As soon as he could turned out to be seventy-three minutes, not that I really noticed because I was asleep for at least sixty of them.

He wasn't alone when he came back though, there was an older man accompanying him and the young doctor looked very sheepish, as if he had done something very wrong and was being taught the error of his ways.

'Good evening, Herr Schneider. My name is Hans Stromberg. I'm one of the senior clinicians here. I'm afraid my young colleague had managed to mix your samples with something else.' Behind him, the young doctor looked thoroughly embarrassed. 'Do you happen to know what blood type you are, Herr Schneider?'

'A Positive,' I replied automatically.

Doctor Stromberg nodded and smiled. 'I'm afraid we will need to take a fresh set of samples, Herr Schneider.'

I pursed my lips. 'I'm just here to see my wife. Visiting hours will be over soon and I have a flight early tomorrow morning.'

He nodded along as I spoke, showing his understanding. 'Yes. I can assure you all haste will be given to this set of samples, Herr Schneider. I think we can have results in under fifteen minutes. That should give you an hour with your wife before they need to close the ward.'

He was doing his best for me and I didn't want to rage at the junior doctor; everyone makes a mistake sometime. 'Let's get on with it then,' I said as I rolled up my sleeve again.

True to his word, and before my eyes could get heavy and close once more, Doctor Stromberg returned. He had the junior doctor with him again, but this time instead of two doctors, there were five and Doctor Stromberg looked... worried. I didn't like it, but the dominant expression on his face was concern.

'What is it?' I asked, leaning forward in my chair to get up as they approached.

Stromberg waved me back down. 'Please don't get up, Herr Schneider. Have you been out of the country recently?'

'Why? What do I have?' a brief fluttering of concern quelled when I realised that I hadn't been anywhere recently and then came back as full-blown panic when I remembered my little excursion to the immortal realm.

'Have you been out of the country?' he prompted again.

'No. I haven't left Germany in years.' It was technically true. 'What's wrong with my blood?'

Doctor Stromberg glanced at one of his colleagues, who all bore the same look of professional concern. Apart from the junior doctor, who mostly looked relieved that he hadn't made a mistake after all.

What Stromberg said made my blood run cold though. 'Herr Schneider. It's not *your* blood.' Seeing that I needed a little more information than that, he added, 'The A Positive blood cells are there, but you have other blood cells as well. And, ah... they are not of any known blood type. Your body should be attacking them, but it isn't.'

My mind reeled from the information, but I had an instant answer for what they were and how they got there. It wasn't one I could share with the doctors or anyone else and I wasn't sure I had it right myself. A question swam to the front of my brain. 'Blood cells have a limited life span, right? So, won't they all die off and be replaced by new blood cells that my body produces?'

Doctor Stromberg frowned as he thought how to answer. 'Herr Schneider, in order for the foreign cells to be in your body right now, your body has to be producing them. It has to be producing both types of blood cells and that's not possible.'

I blinked a few times, unable to work out what I was supposed to say next.

I started to get up, meeting Doctor Stromberg's hands as he tried to convince me to stay seated. 'Herr Schneider we are going to admit you. It is imperative that we find out what is causing this and treat it. Your symptoms at this time do not appear to be life-threatening but they are also not consistent with what we are seeing in your blood.'

I stood up anyway, forcing him backward as I filled the space where he wanted to be. 'I'm sorry. I have to go.'

His arm came up to bar me. 'Herr Schneider I really must advise against leaving this hospital.'

I grabbed his hand and shook it. 'Duly noted, doc. It is not tenable for me to remain here at this time. If my symptoms worsen, I will return.'

There were several more cautionary words as I put my coat and scarf back on. I wasn't really listening; my brain was too full of other thoughts to hear what he had to say. I didn't get to see Kerstin and I wasn't sure whether they would let me in tomorrow either. Regardless of that, I was leaving.

Outside the hospital's main entrance, I grabbed the first taxi in a line of four and as he took me home, I thought about what was happening inside my body.

Chapter 11

Did the word infected fit my circumstances? I wasn't sure that it did, but I couldn't come up with another one that worked better. There were blood cells inside my body that were not of any known human blood type. So, what were they, you might ask? The answer, I told myself, was demon.

I defeated Teague a few days ago by superheating the water in every cell of his body until it exploded. An atomised mist burst outward from him, but it wasn't just a liquid spray, it had been carried by a pulse wave of magical energy which hit the other two beings in the room with him: me and Zachary.

There was no way to prove it, but I was convinced the weird blood cells and the fact that I felt awful were entirely due to me absorbing some of the magical essence of the demon. I had no idea what that meant though. Was I going to become a demon now? Was I going to die? What was a demon anyway? I knew next to nothing about them, but the impression was that they were a separate race. Edward Blake had talked about the realms splitting, or was that Daniel? I couldn't remember, but if the two realms had once been one, then it stood to reason that the demons had lived on Earth with man. Teague said he had familiars before and was upset at being denied one for so long. Didn't he say it had been thousands of years? I had to assume that meant they enslaved us, but if they could wield magic and we couldn't, then it stood to reason that they would rule over us. How come no one knew anything about this? How had it been lost to history?

I coughed in the back of the taxi, my breath catching as I went into a fit of coughing and couldn't stop for half a minute. The driver flicked his eyes up at the rear-view mirror, probably just to make sure I wasn't going to ruin his night by dying in the back of his cab. When I stopped and caught my breath again, he focused back on the road. I half expected to see blood on my hands where I had been covering my mouth yet there was none.

The driver was moving cautiously through the city streets. Snow was falling again; fat white flakes being swept from the windshield to build up at the left-hand edge. He would need to clean it off by hand when we stopped, which he did once I had given him a note and told him to keep the change.

I didn't feel like sleeping. Honestly, I was worried about whether I would die in the night or turn into a new form of hybrid human/demon abomination. That very thought occurred to me as I sat on the edge of my bed to take off my shoes and an answer to the city's werewolf problem hit me: I was feeling all manner of unpleasant symptoms but nothing terrible had occurred yet. But what about Zachary? He was a shapeshifter, a werewolf, and one thing was for sure, he was very different physiologically to me. So, if I was suffering because I got a magical burst of demon juice that was somehow changing me physically, what had it done to him?

I called Heike. 'Otto? It's after midnight, you torturous pig, why are you phoning me when you should be sleeping?'

'Has there been anything back from the search for Zachary?' I blurted, ignoring her question completely. His picture was on the news and getting circulated to police precincts everywhere. Sooner or later, someone was going to see him.

'Not a thing,' she replied. 'Why? I thought you were convinced he was innocent.'

I puffed out my cheeks and made an exasperated sound. 'I did. I do... I don't know. Something happened when I made Teague explode and I think it might have affected him.'

'Affected him how?'

'I don't know that either.' I could sense that she was about to call me some more names, so I headed her off by telling her about my blood and about what I thought that might mean.

'You think he could be completely out of control?' she asked. I could hear that the idea scared her, and she was right to be frightened. Zachary would be dangerous in human form; he was tall and strong and deadly looking. Add werewolf power and razor-sharp claws plus a supernatural ability to shake off injury and you had a creature that was going to be very hard to stop.

'It would explain why he would attack people so soon after risking his life to help a group he had no connection or allegiance to.' I felt saddened by the idea that the killer we were hunting might be the man I met just a few days ago, but I could no longer rule it out.

'How are you feeling?' she asked.

My brain was wandering, and I took a second to answer; I had thought of something else while we were talking. 'Tired,' I replied around a yawn. I bade her goodnight, apologised for disturbing her sleep and promised to see her at the airport for coffee and breakfast at 0400hrs.

'I'll collect you. You are a mite unreliable at the moment and I don't want to be waiting around for you. Besides, if you drop dead in the night I might not have to go.'

Great joke.

We both hung up and I finally took off my second shoe. How to kill him? That was the thought that randomly occurred to me. Could I find a way to subdue him while in his werewolf state? Or would it be possible to find a way to force him to transform back to human form? How would I do that? Was the moon even a factor?

I fell asleep fully clothed with images of the sun and the moon in my head and dreamed I was a demon with Katja as my slave, bound and on a leash at my feet. It wasn't a nice dream and I snapped awake around two in the morning, finally undressing and climbing back beneath the covers. I still felt like crap though and sleep eluded me, which meant I got to prove Heike wrong about my reliability because I was dressed and showered and ready to go when Heike's car pulled up outside my house.

I was going to the Czech Republic.

Chapter 12

The roads were already clear at 0330hrs when we set off from my house, the super-efficient German gritters out in force as we made our way out of the city to the airport. Heike was good enough to comment that I looked ready to die. Apparently, my skin had taken on an ashen pallor, which when one added the bags under my eyes from lack of sleep, made me look like a zombie she said.

'They might not let you on the flight, you know.'

At this very point I didn't want to get on the stupid flight anyway. I wanted to go back to my house and eat some of the luxury food items I bought in preparation for no longer having access to them. Then I wanted to sleep for a week. I didn't say that though. What I said was, 'If we can get an item of the missing girl's clothing, I can invoke my tracking spell and might be able to find her body. That would give the family some peace and would make the trip feel worthwhile.'

Unable to argue, Heike nodded. 'I still think we should improve your chances of getting on the flight.'

'How do you propose to do that?'

'Make up.' I raised an eyebrow. 'I'll just improve your colour slightly. Make you look less like a walking infection zone.' I wanted to argue but knew it would be churlish to do so; she was only trying to help. I shrugged and let her walk me to a corner of the airport lounge where she dabbed some foundation on my face.

'What's that?' I asked as she put the foundation thing away and held up a thick brown pencil.

'Eyebrow pencil,' she explained as if it was obvious.

I held up a hand to fend her off. 'That's quite enough feminine products for one day.'

'Don't be such a girl, Otto. I'm just trying to tidy you up a bit.'

'The foundation will have to suffice. Let's get through security and get some breakfast.' I think she had been trying to use the eyebrow pencil just to see if I would let her, rather than because I needed it, the woman making her own entertainment at my expense.

Security, boarding and the flight itself passed without incident, Heike falling asleep with her head lolling onto my shoulder almost before we were off the runway. I managed a little sleep too, but the trip was so short the plane was coming down no sooner than it had gone up and we were back on the ground and in Brno.

It was a city I had never visited before and I doubted I would ever find reason to visit again. Located towards the west of the Czech Republic, it was supposed to have an ancient and attractive city centre, which most European cities could boast, but we wouldn't get to see any of that.

'Detective Dressler?' A man holding a cardboard sign with *Dressler* written on it stood right outside the arrivals doors. He must have had her photograph as well because he recognised her instantly. As we crossed to him, avoiding a mother with four small children who were mostly out of control, he held out his hand to shake. 'Good morning, I'm Detective Josef Porizkova. I hope your flight was okay.'

Heike shook his hand. 'It was fine, thank you. And thank you for being here to meet us at such short notice. This is my colleague Otto Schneider. He is a special consultant working with the Bremen police on this series of murders.'

Josef swung his head around to greet me and his expression froze. I could see him looking at my face and I knew he was checking out my makeup. He caught himself doing it, cast his eyes away and back again, this time looking at my eyes and not the daft foundation

Heike convinced me to wear. I could feel her trying not to snigger. We shook hands and exchanged pleasantries, and then we were moving again, following him to a carpark. He was to be our escort for the day, assigned as a courtesy by his chief, who, it seemed, knew Chief Muller back in Bremen from somewhere.

'Do you believe the murders to be linked?' he asked as he paid for the parking ticket.

Like any good police officer, Heike gave him a noncommittal answer. 'Too early to tell.'

'There are lots of similarities though,' he continued. 'Murders this brutal are rare. Murder here is rare anyway, especially out of the city and when we do get one, it is either a cheating husband getting caught by his wife or a drunken bar brawl with a bad ending. A double murder in the countryside is unheard of. To me, a serial killer who then moves on, sounds quite believable.'

Picking up on his comment, Heike asked, 'The second body, that of the girl, hasn't been found yet, has it?' She was riding up front leaving me in the back. I couldn't remember the last time I had ridden in the back of a car and it made me feel like a child out for the day with mum and dad up front.

Josef chuckled. 'You're right. I'm calling it a double murder but without the body she is still classed as missing. We had officers in from all over the country, hundreds of them to search the fields and farm buildings. Divers came in to explore the lakes and rivers, but we haven't found any sign of her. Just a few specs of her blood and her clothing at the site where we found her poor uncle.

Heike made no comment. He was driving us out of the city, the size of the buildings getting smaller and smaller as industrial units gave way to houses and then to open fields.

I leaned forward to speak to Josef, 'Will we be going to her house?'

'Zuzana's house?' he questioned. 'I wasn't planning to. My instructions were to take you to the crime scene and then show you all the evidence we have at the crime lab. None of us could work out why you wanted to come here, if I am honest. We could have emailed all the evidence just as easily. In fact, we did do, just yesterday afternoon when DS Schenk asked for it. He said your flights were already booked though.'

Heike made no comment. That Schenk had sent us here for no good reason was obvious but there was nothing to be gained by showing the discord between the Bremen officers.

'Why do you want to go to her house?' he asked, then added another question before I could answer. 'Sorry, Otto, I should have asked what your speciality is. They obviously hired you for a reason.'

His question gave me the opening I wanted. 'I specialise in finding missing persons. I need to go to her house, specifically her room so I can get a feel for who she was.' Actually, I needed to go to her room to find a piece of clothing she had worn. Such things carry an echo of the person and can be used to make a link to the owner. A pillowcase would do it, provided it hadn't been washed. Would her mother have done the laundry for her missing daughter? Dirty clothes worked much better than clean ones.

Josef glanced at me in his mirror. 'That sounds all rather mysterious. Are you suggesting a spiritual connection?'

I couldn't tell if he was yanking my chain or genuinely believed in abilities beyond that which he could see. Heike jumped in though, 'You just have to trust that he needs to get to her room. Wherever she is, Otto is a *wizard* at finding missing people.' She smirked at her own joke, risking a quick glance at me and smirked even more when I cut my eyes at her.

Josef didn't argue. Instead, he put his turn signal on and took the next left. 'Their farm is this way. In fact,' he ducked down to squint out of Heike's window, 'if you look through those trees, it's the building next to the large while silo.'

We both looked. The farm was a couple of kilometres away, a speck on the landscape at this point but it wouldn't take long to get there.

Which it didn't. As we neared the house, Heike and I started pulling on gloves and scarves again, having shed them in the warmth of the car. Ahead was a woman, dressed to be indoors, not out, but throwing food for some chickens in her yard. She had just turned around to go back into the house when she saw us pull in.

She looked to be in her late thirties, kind of thick about the hips but a stout woman who performed physical tasks for a living. Her blonde hair was plaited to hang both sides of her head. It was tidy but the style was clearly functional, like her outfit; designed to do its job which was to protect the wearer and keep her warm, not make her look good.

She recognised Josef and came to his window. 'Detective Porizkova, is there any news?' To me it seemed like she had already accepted the worst but was still clinging to a glimmer of hope because her daughter's body was yet to be found. She waited for his answer, holding her breath and fearing what he was going to say.

'I'm afraid not, Ivana. I wish I could give you better news. I'm here because there have been more murders.' She took the news without emotion, either because all emotion had been beaten out of her already, or perhaps because she didn't care about anyone else; she just wanted to hear about her little girl. 'This is Detective Lieutenant Heike Dressler from Bremen.'

'German?' she queried.

'Yes, Ivana. There have been two killings there in the last few days.'

'I heard about them on the news. Is it the same person?'

'That's what we are hoping to work out,' replied Heike, leaning across into Josef's space to answer.

Ivana blinked but didn't question her. 'What can I do to help? That's why you are here.'

Ignored thus far in the back of the car, I opened my door and got out. 'Ivana,' I spoke softly in getting her attention, 'my name is Otto Schneider. I specialise in finding missing people. I hope that I can find your daughter and that doing so will help the police to find the killer. Will you show me her room?'

She didn't question my request, choosing to turn and head toward her house and the warmth in response. I hurried after her, Heike and Josef jumping out of the car to catch up with me.

The farmhouse had a centuries old look; rough-hewn chunks of rock for the first metre of the wall before it became red house bricks. The windows were small, and they were not double glazed which must have let the cold in, but inside the house it was warm, and it was modern. There were new appliances throughout the kitchen, and I spied a wide plasma screen in a nook through a door to my left.

Ivana went into the kitchen, depositing the eggs and placing the bucket with the chicken feed to one side. A large black cat strolled across the room and rubbed against my legs. I looked down at it with my second sight, smiling to myself that cats had a supernatural aura unlike any other creature I ever saw.

I had to kill the smile though, the woman's daughter was missing and almost certainly dead. So certainly, in fact, that it felt foolhardy to not consider it a double murder as Josef did. Once the eggs were away, Ivana cleaned her hands, shook them a few times and dried them on her pinafore. 'It's this way,' she said, not making eye contact as she walked between the three of us.

Josef made to accompany me, but Heike put an arm in his way. 'He works better alone.' Heike knew what I was going to do and how I would do it. No one else needed to see me going through a young woman's dirty laundry basket.

'Please don't touch anything,' Ivana begged as she stopped outside a door that was clearly one that led to a girl's bedroom. It still bore the princess framed name plate on the outside of the door, leftovers from her childhood no one had got around to removing or replacing yet. 'I want it to look how she left it when she returns.'

I couldn't break her bubble of delusion, so I lied through my teeth as I promised to not touch anything and was glad I was the only one in the house that could tell when someone wasn't being truthful. She left me, going back downstairs without even opening the door to her daughter's bedroom. The door wasn't locked, I couldn't think why it would be, so I went inside and looked around. I didn't need to see her bedroom at all, of course. What I needed was to find an item of her clothing. An obvious laundry hamper got my hopes up, but it was empty, not a scrap of clothing in it. It was bad news, and when I sniffed the bed, I could tell it was clean; freshly laundered and another dead end.

I wasn't busted yet; I could always use an item of jewellery because trinkets held an echo. Emotional attachment probably caused it, but it wasn't as strong as an item of clothing would be, so if the body was buried or it had been taken far away, the signal might be too faint to work. This wasn't my first rodeo though, or whatever the expression was. I assumed it was an American saying but I could be mistaken. Carefully kneeling, keeping my movements light, I bent down to look under the bed. It's a universal truth that people do not clean under their beds and teenagers are more guilty than most, so it was with no surprise that I found a forgotten pair of panties when I carefully pulled the bed away from the wall.

There was no good reason for me to feel uncomfortable about stuffing a young woman's soiled panties into my pocket; I had no ill-thoughts, no sexual drivers for such an action. I just needed an item of her clothing and they were what I found.

Back downstairs, I offered Heike the barest of nods to let her know that I found what I needed. Her eyes reflected acknowledgement; she knew it was a good thing for me to be able to find the girl's body, both for the investigation and for the family. There was nothing further I needed here, and I had a strong desire to leave so I could invoke the tracking spell and begin the quest. However, decorum prevented me from heading directly for the door.

'Did you find what you need?' asked Josef, his tone curious but with no sense of irony or anything else hidden in subtext.

'I did.'

He moved toward the door instantly. 'We should leave Mrs Brychta in peace then.' Was he anxious to leave because he was uncomfortable being here or was he aware that Ivana really didn't want us in her house? I would never know but it felt likely to be the latter since she kept her back to us almost the whole time as we filed to her door, turning to bid us a cursory goodbye only at the last possible moment.

He went to the car, but I didn't follow him which made Heike pause as well. On one knee with my gloves still in my pockets, I fished out my old, broken compass, the one I

73

used for tracking spells. I had it with me today unlike the last time I needed it, confidence brimming this time because I was doing familiar spells with familiar tools.

Josef made it to the car before he noticed we weren't with him, spinning around to look for us and seeing me messing around on the ground. I paid no attention, but I could feel his curious expression as much as I could see it.

Pulling an air spell into my hand made his eyebrows rise; not that he could see it of course, an air spell is just as invisible as air however he could see that I was doing something and that it was disturbing the dirt on the ground around me. It made him come back.

'What's going on?' he asked.

I didn't answer, so Heike did. Somewhat unhelpfully, it turned out. 'He's conjuring a tracking spell.'

Josef said nothing for a moment, waiting for her punchline no doubt. When it didn't come, he smiled and chuckled. 'Like a magician?'

My eyes narrowed all by themselves, though my voice was calm and detached when I said, 'Magicians are children's entertainers.'

'So, what are you? A wizard?' he was almost laughing at the idea. 'Can you do that thing when you vanish in a puff of smoke?'

To shut him up, I dropped the air spell I needed to perform the tracking spell and conjured fire into my right hand which I then threw with my left hand to control it. I can't deny a temptation to blow out one of the tyres on his car so he would have to change it for the spare but that seemed a little extreme. I settled for the base of a tree, the result much akin to the flare from a flame thrower if a person pulled the trigger for a second and let go.

Josef uttered some choice expletives as he jumped back in shock. 'What the hell was that?' he cried.

I had already doused the fire spell and reconjured the air spell I needed. Heike moved to intercept Josef, but both stopped when I fished the teenage girl's knickers from my pocket. It wasn't like I could hide what they were; the pair I found were bright pink and had a thong string at the back and a lace trim across the top. They were sex wear; not really the thing I would want my teenage daughter wearing if I had one.

Blocking out all distractions, such as Heike arguing with Josef who was getting upset, I pulled air to direct the spell and sent it to find Zuzana. The compass spun and pulled, funnelling through her garment to determine where she was and choosing a distinct direction. It was faint though; I could tell without question that she wasn't anywhere near us. In fact, I would guess that she was hundreds of kilometres away. It explained why the local searches hadn't found her.

Now that the spell was done, and I knew she wasn't close, I stood up straight again which acted as a trigger for Josef to resume his agitated state. 'Hey, what the hell was that burst of flame? How did you do that?' He moved in toward me, his eyes on my sleeves as if he expected to find a small portable flamethrower hidden up one.

I took a step back so he couldn't crowd me and showed him my empty sleeves. His eyes flicked up to mine. 'It's not a trick,' I assured him.

Just behind him, Heike added, 'It's really not.'

'Then what is it?' he demanded, anger dominating his face though he tried to keep it in check. He felt like he was being conned somehow. 'Are you going to tell me it is magic?' He was trying not to sneer and failing.

This wasn't the first time I had revealed myself. I was doing it more and more now, partly because there was suddenly so much more supernatural activity than I had ever experienced and partly because the thing with Daniel hung over my head and I just didn't seem to care anymore if people knew what I was.

I asked him a question. 'What do you think killed Jan Brychta?

'What do I... don't you mean who?' His brow wrinkled as he tried to find hidden meaning in my question.

'His body was torn apart. We have two bodies in the same condition in Bremen. We are not searching for a man.'

Josef argued, 'DNA from saliva found on his wounds is human. He was killed by a man.'

Despite suspecting that I was probably wasting my time, I pressed ahead anyway. 'He was killed by a werewolf.'

Heike's phone rang and she answered it just as Josef burst out laughing. 'You really had me there for a moment. You should be on the stage,' he chuckled. 'You are totally convincing.'

Heike made a show of taking the phone away from her ear so she could speak to us. 'They've found three more cases that look to be the same killer.' Both of us looked her way. 'Two in Prague and another one in Leipzig.'

I drew a map in my head. 'That's a straight line from Brno to Bremen.'

Josef nodded. 'When were the bodies found?'

Heike was talking on the phone again, wrapping up the conversation so we had to wait for her to finish before he got an answer. 'The one in Leipzig was found eight days ago but had been dead several days by then. A known pimp just like the lowlifes killed in Bremen. He was robbed too and partly eaten. The ones in Prague were found last night but had been dead for approximately ten days. They found a man and a young woman in the boot of his car. Same thing though; wallet and jewellery lifted, and their bodies ripped to shreds. They haven't managed to ID any of them yet, but Schenk and the others are liaising with them. This is fast becoming an international man hunt. Your friend Zachary is still the number one suspect.'

Josef blinked at Heike. 'Zachary Barnabus? We got the picture of him yesterday. You know him?'

The question was aimed at me, but Heike answered, 'We both do. Has the picture been circulated? If he was here someone would remember him; he's a huge bear of a man, far too memorable to be forgotten in the couple of weeks since the murder and utterly unable to blend into a crowd.'

Josef looked uncertain. 'I don't know. I was assigned to other tasks and then sent to collect you from the airport this morning.'

'Well, get on it, man.' Heike filled her voice with frustration. 'Get on your radio and find out. Get a photograph sent to your tablet and show it to Mrs Brychta. If we can prove he was here, we can be almost certain that he is the killer.'

As Josef dashed to the car to check in and get a copy of the picture, I told Heike, 'We need to get to Prague.'

'Why?'

'The tracking spell is pulling us that way. It might be that the killer took the girl with him. The signal is really faint, so she is many kilometres from here, but she could be in Prague.'

'You think she might be alive?' Heike asked, her expression telling me she didn't agree.

I shrugged. 'I would rather find her alive, but I have no influence over that.'

Josef dashed back from the car, jogging straight by us to knock on Ivana's door. We let him get on with it, discussing our next move until he returned just a minute later.

'She's never seen him before. The farms here are so spread out though that he could have worked at one nearby as a casual helper and she would never have seen him. I need to show his picture around and see if he was taken on anywhere nearby.'

'That's a good idea, Josef,' Heike agreed. 'We need to move on though.'

'Yes, I was supposed to be taking you to the site where we found the body.'

She looked at me, so I nodded, answering her question to confirm the course of action we had just discussed. 'That's no longer necessary. We don't need to go to the station either since the team already sent all the evidence to our team in Bremen. Can you take us to the airport?'

Chapter 13

At the airport we hired a car, a process that took about eight minutes, a valid driver's licence, and a credit card. When we had been waiting for Josef outside Ivana's house, I proposed to Heike that we forget Schenk's order to return as quickly as we could and look instead for the missing girl. The total distance by road all the way back to Bremen was around eight hundred kilometres and could be done in around eight hours so we could beat the intended flight back there if we didn't find reason to stop along the way, which, to be honest, I believed we would.

With me driving and the satnav guiding us, Heike made a call to Klaus Nieswand. His voice came through the speaker on her phone. 'Detective Nieswand.'

'Klaus, it's Heike. Can you be overheard?'

We got a moment of silence from his end. I imagined him checking around and possibly moving to sit somewhere else. 'No. What do you need?'

I listened as she talked. 'Klaus, I'm not sure who we can trust within that group. Schenk sent us here for no reason at all; he got all the evidence gathered in Brno sent by data transfer yesterday.'

'Yes, it's all here. They had me going through it all night.' To prove a point he yawned, the sound of him trying to stifle it obvious.

'We're not coming back, Klaus. Otto thinks he can find the missing girl from the murder here, so we are pushing on to Prague. If she is alive, she might be able to tell us who the murderer is.'

He didn't respond for a second and when he did, he was whispering. 'Look, we are all under orders not to tell you this, but Zachary was spotted here last night.' Heike and I exchanged glances. 'Schenk doesn't want you to know because he thinks Otto is able to contact him and might be helping him avoid the police.' Of course he did, the utter moron.

'Is the sighting reliable?' asked Heike.

'Only as reliable as they ever are. It was one guy that saw him, down at the docks again, right by where we chased the wolf thing a few hours before. Schenk said he was returning to the scene of the crime.' This wasn't good. Zachary had been very clear about his need to leave the city because crowds of people drove him a bit crazy. Add to that the demon magic coursing through his body... I had to accept that he was probably still in Bremen and the murderous creature we were chasing might well be a man I considered an ally.

'Are the Bureau telling you anything? Are they helping?' I asked.

'Not really,' Klaus snorted. 'That bunch are as secretive as you can get. Voss just listens all the time, he never says anything. The beat cops are going out in double patrols now and there are extra cops arriving every day. We got four from some village called Wertag last night. I had to look it up on a map; it's six hours south of here, right down by the Alps. Suddenly Bremen is a hot spot for murder and there's a lot of talk about supernatural stuff and the end of the world.'

'What do you mean?' asked Heike.

'Too many cops have seen the shilt now. The battle with Edward Blake outside your house was seen by yet more cops and last night six of them saw what they described as an impossibly tall wolf walking on its back legs. Schenk is treating it like a joke, but the word werewolf is being used by half the people here and there's a junket of press outside the station demanding answers. Add it all up and people think there's some kind of biblical end of the world event starting. It's getting scary here.'

'We're on our way back,' I assured him. 'Don't hide this conversation from Schenk, okay? There's no need to include yourself in our lie. Tell him we were in contact, that we don't trust him, and we are trying to find the missing girl.' Asking Klaus to lie for us would just create trouble for him, trouble we could handle for ourselves.

When she ended the call, Heike stared out of the windscreen at the autobahn ahead. She seemed agitated now. 'We need to get back to Bremen.'

'We do,' I agreed. 'We also need to follow up on what we have.' I fished in my pocket for the broken compass and placed it on my left thigh. It was pointing dead ahead. 'She's in this direction. So, we are heading to Bremen right now and also heading toward the girl.'

'Or her body,' murmured Heike.

I didn't argue. Finding her body might be important too. Silence filled the car for the next hundred kilometres as the distance to Prague ticked down. Just less than two hours after picking the car up, we were heading into the city outskirts, the autobahn skirting right by the central business district.

I already knew Zuzana wasn't here because the compass wanted me to go on and the signal itself was still weak. Did we stop though? Could we learn anything by examining the evidence here?

'It won't take long,' Heike said when I asked her thoughts. 'Schenk will find out that we didn't take the flight and will try to cause trouble for us. This won't help my hearing tomorrow, but I would think the least we can expect is for him to demand we get taken off the case. At least this way, we can get to see the evidence we won't see back in Bremen.'

It was a solid argument and it only took her one phone call to get connected with an opposite number at the Prague police HQ. Like most of Europe, everyone is multilingual, though the Czechs' could thank the Nazi invasion for their fluent German ability. Nevertheless, despite speaking only a few words of Czech between us, we were able to converse in our native tongue and get through to the lead officer on the case here.

Ten minutes later, he was meeting us in the carpark of the police HQ as I pulled the rental car into a parking space.

'You're having quite the time of it in Bremen,' he said as we were getting out of the car. A chill wind was whipping across the car park, making me instantly cold after the warmth of the car. Detective Inspector Vlasta Voskovec wore a shirt and thin sweater; enough for inside where he was working no doubt but too little to be outside for long. Maybe he thought he could tough it out for a minute or so, but I could see how keen he was to get back inside. 'It's all over the news,' he added. 'A whole run of murders recently.'

'And that's why we are here,' replied Heike.

Vlasta had his hands tucked into his armpits to stop them from freezing but offered his right to shake as Heike got to him and again as I rounded the car. Introductions had been done over the phone, but we did them again now, Vlasta pausing to examine my face when he got to me. 'Are you alright, Herr Schneider? You look quite unwell.'

'It's Otto, please. And yes, I am alright. It's just a winter cold.'

He nodded rather than argue and we found ourselves staring at each other, each of us trying to be polite and waiting for someone else to talk.

A heartbeat later, and just before I did it myself, Vlasta grabbed the impetus, 'God it's cold out here. Let's get inside.'

Chapter 14

The police headquarters in Prague was sleek and modern, looking every bit like the headquarters of a large and successful corporation, not a municipal service that made no profit. Quite how much taxpayers' money had gone into it, I couldn't guess, but the entrance was lined with a marble floor and had, at its centre, a statue of a cop helping a little girl which had to be three metres tall. It served no purpose from which the citizens could benefit except maybe to make the cops feel more inclined to be good at their jobs.

Vlasta led us through the wide atrium and to a bank of elevators. The elevators, their housing and shaft were made of glass or Perspex so we were like fish in a bowl and could see out into all the open plan offices as the car ascended.

'Here we are,' he announced. 'The serious crimes division. My division,' he told us proudly. 'We have a very high success rate for closing cases with a conviction. The highest in the country, in fact,' he boasted.

'That's most impressive,' acknowledged Heike since he was clearly fishing for compliments and we needed his help. She was patient also as he led us into his department and started to show us around. He wanted to show off his baby, but we didn't have time.

'Sorry,' I interrupted his flow. 'We're on a tight clock, I'm afraid. Can we get to the evidence?'

He grinned ruefully. 'Sorry. I have a habit of getting carried away.' He tapped the interactive desk he had just been about to show us and looked disappointed to not show it off when he took us across the room. Making a beeline for a man and a woman working together at another desk, he called to get their attention. 'Karol, Tereza.'

A man and a woman stood up from the desk they were bent over and turned our way. Like Rugler and Moltz they were both in their early thirties and attractive looking. Both gave off a serious, professional vibe that suggested they would be successful no matter what career they chose.

'This is Otto and Heike from Bremen,' he introduced us. 'They are working what appears to be the same case there.'

'Have you been able to identify either of the victims?' Heike asked.

The woman, Tereza, answered. 'The man was easy enough. The car turned out to be his which allowed us to track his driver's licence to make a positive ID. His body is torn up, but his face was mostly untouched.' She turned around to the table behind her, the whole top surface of which was an interactive screen. I had seen such things on television but never in person. She used it like a phone, swiping and moving files and apps about to bring the dead man's picture to the screen, then enlarged it. 'This is Ivan Chýlková, aged sixty-three. A construction worker originally from Brno, he moved to Prague three years ago. Nothing outstanding or surprising about him that we can see.'

'What about the girl?' I asked.

Tereza swiped at the tabletop again, a fresh picture appearing next to Ivan's. It wasn't her driver's licence picture though; it was a shot from the crime scene. There were spots of blood on her face and in her hair. The days spent in the boot of the car had not done her any good, decomposition setting in already and the skin beginning to look quite ashen as the fluids inside settled at the lowest point of her body. Only the cold would have preserved her this well; in the summer it would be much worse this long after death. She looked to be in her early twenties, but it was impossible to tell with so much damage and decay. 'The cause of death appears to be massive blood loss. She was torn in half across her stomach, her internal organs had spilled out,' Tereza explained emotionlessly. We are cross referencing missing persons to see if we can work out who she is. The obvious guess is that she was a sex worker and that was why she was with the old man.'

Heike turned to me. 'Is there anything you can do to identify her? Some kind of reverse tracking thing to take you back to where she lives?'

I shook my head. 'No.' In truth I had never tried to work a spell that way, but I didn't think it would be possible anyway. A piece of clothing held an echo of the person, but I couldn't envisage a way to take a piece of the dead person to track backwards to a house or an apartment.

Vlasta looked at Heike confused. 'I'm sorry, what were you asking?'

Heike ignored his question rather than introduce the concept of magic. 'How sure are you about the time of death?'

It was Tereza who answered again, 'The medical examiner said it might shift by a day either way, but he seemed fairly sure. The cold preserved them, but he could allow for that in his calculations.'

'So, ten days?' she attempted to confirm. Tereza nodded. It left Zachary still in the frame for the murders. Heike had the same thought. 'Have you had any hits in the search for Zachary Barnabus?

This time it was her partner who spoke. 'Nothing yet. His picture has been circulated and put out on the news. But it's a big city with a lot of tourists. A large percentage of the people who were here ten days ago have already moved on. He might have been here but whether anyone ever comes forward to report it is anyone's guess.'

I thought of something. 'Heike what do you know about the victim in Leipzig?'

Tereza answered for her, turning to the table again to swipe around until she found the file she wanted. 'We have it all here.' Another man's face appeared on the screen. 'His name was Hermann Zimmermann. He was a pimp with a stable of girls. There are multiple arrests on his record, the most recent was earlier this year for possession of marijuana but he was released without charge. I think we can assume he is part of a larger operation and had protection somewhere.'

'Not anymore,' I murmured.

Heike squinted her eyes at me. 'What are you thinking, Otto?'

I pointed to the face on the table. 'The two victims in Bremen were both in the game of exploiting women. So was this guy. That feels like a very targeted demographic to me. Then we have Ivan in the boot of his car with a much younger woman. If we assume she is a prostitute, that makes him her customer for the night. I would guess that the girl interrupted the murder or otherwise got in the way and that caused her death. The odd one out here is Jan Brychta. He wasn't killed in the city and he isn't involved in the sex game. That we know of,' I added for correctness.

Karol agreed, 'We really need to know who the girl is, but you may be onto something. The killer is robbing people and cutting them to shreds, leaving their bodies covered in saliva which suggests some kind of sex fetish act is driving the murders. If the killer is trying to fulfil a fantasy, then the stealing is after the fact and just a convenience because the money is there.'

'There's a lot of ifs here,' Heike pointed out.

She wasn't wrong but I couldn't shift the feeling that we were onto something. 'Jan Brychta still has nothing in common with the other victims. Even if we believe the girl was targeted deliberately and the old man got in the way, it is still the sex industry that links them all.'

We talked it around for an hour, agreeing and disagreeing, sharing ideas and looking at evidence. There wasn't all that much of it despite the number of crime scenes which had now been catalogued. The saliva was the same at every scene, that was one thing, but there were no fingerprints and the only hair which was not from the victims was identified as wolf hair. Heike and I kept quiet at that point, having learned our lesson in Bremen. Had the werewolf still been here and likely to cause further deaths, I would have warned them and quietened their ridicule by displaying my magic. As it was, the danger had passed for this city, so we said nothing.

Outside the sun was setting and both Heike and I were yawning. 'We should push on,' I told her, announcing to the team our intention to leave.

'I need some sleep, Otto,' she managed around another yawn.

'We need to push on,' I argued, leaning in closer to her ear so I could whisper, 'Bremen is in danger. I don't think anyone other than me can stop him.' It was the first time I had admitted to her that it might be Zachary.

She couldn't argue with the need to get back, so we compromised and agreed to push on with me driving. We would cover as much distance as possible and finish the journey off in the morning. Plus, there was the need to follow the tracking spell to find Zuzana; the slim hope that she might still be alive demanding that we waste as little time as possible.

We thanked Heike's Czech colleagues and let Vlasta escort us back to our car where the temperature had dropped another ten degrees. He was shivering the moment we all stepped outside, Heike and I already had our coats on though, the outside temperature too low to wait for the car to warm up. We waved him off at the door, shaking his hand and wishing him luck.

Though we didn't know it when we set off, we had already seen the vital clue. Not that we could have stopped the events about to unfold in Bremen even if we had realised what it was.

Chapter 15

The unfamiliar roads out of Prague were clogged, the first ten kilometres of our journey taking as long as the next one hundred. We made reasonable time though once we were clear of the congestion, passing through the border without slowing down and powering back into what was East Germany before the wall came down.

The car ate up the kilometres, but I knew we couldn't make it back without stopping. I hadn't got much sleep last night and was already tired when we left Prague just before four o'clock. We had six hundred kilometres to cover back to Bremen which would take at least four hours, the hold up in rush hour school traffic adding an hour before we had even really started.

I was in a hurry, but not at the expense of safety. Our plan was to go as far as we could and then stop for some sleep, setting off early the following morning to get back to Bremen for breakfast. Heike was asleep in the car before I hit the Prague outskirts.

By the time I got to Leipzig I was flagging, and halfway to Magdeburg, I knew I was done. I kept going a little longer, my eyes heavy and my body weary, but I wasn't actually falling asleep so there was no danger to other drivers or indeed to myself or Heike. I twitched the wheel deliberately to wake Heike up when we were ten kilometres from Magdeburg. It was a big enough place for us to be able to find a small hotel with a restaurant nearby. A few hours sleep would see me right.

As Heike came awake, rubbing her eyes and smacking her lips together, I checked my broken compass again. The signal was still weak and still pointing directly ahead. Zuzana, or her body, was still out there, somewhere along this road. It felt weak to stop for sleep when a nineteen-year-old woman might be in mortal danger, but fatigue demanded it.

'Where are we?' Heike asked as she stretched, pushing her ample chest out as she forced her arms back in the confined space.

'Just outside Magdeburg. Can you find us a hotel? One with a restaurant nearby?'

'What kind of food do you want?' she asked around a yawn as she fished out her phone.

'I don't care. I just need to fill my stomach and get a little shut eye.'

She squinted at the clock. 'Have I been out all that time?'

I nodded.

'I didn't snore, did I?

'Not at all,' I lied. She snored so loud I had to wonder if she was part Minotaur.

Halfway through looking up hotels, she said, 'Do you want to just push on to Bremen? We can't have more than two hours to go.'

'Less probably, but I'm beat.'

'I can take over,' she said around another yawn. 'You can get in the back and sleep. I'm fine with that.'

'I need to do the tracking spell as we go. It won't work for you.'

'Oh.' She frowned. 'How about we stop for some food. Fill the fuel tank, set off again and I can wake you once every hour so you can do the spell.' Then as an afterthought, she asked, 'How are you feeling now?'

She clearly wanted to get back and it would mean we both got to sleep in our own beds tonight. It made sense, so even though all I wanted to do was stretch out and go to sleep, I agreed to her proposition. 'I feel about the same as I did; aching and tired and not quite right. It's all minor ailments,' I added so it wouldn't sound like I was trying to make a big deal out of it. 'Let's push on. It makes more sense to get back. We have to stop though; I have needed a restroom since Leipzig.'

Ten minutes later we were walking through the door of an Italian restaurant. I excused myself to visit the restroom while Heike found a table.

Business done, I washed my hands, idly staring into nothing, but when I looked back up, I jumped out of my skin. Daniel was standing behind me.

Fright spun me around, a spell instantly forming in my right hand, but Daniel was faster, a thread of ethereal white energy whipping out from his right hand to ensnare me like a magical lasso. It drew my arms in tight against my body, trapping me.

'Where are you going, Otto?' he asked. 'You wouldn't be foolish enough to try to escape me, would you?'

'What are you talking about?' I managed to squeak as the magical energy lasso around me continued to constrict.

'You were not in Bremen when I looked. You do realise I can find you anywhere, right? Why would you try to run away? You forced me to unleash the shilt again.'

'You did what?' Was he really telling me the shilt were back in Bremen and preying on the population just because I got on a plane? 'I had to go to the Czech Republic, you idiot,' I hissed. 'There's a werewolf tearing up people in Bremen and I need to stop it.'

'Yes, I know of it. The shilt reported it days ago when they encountered it. What does that have to do with the Czech Republic?'

I was beginning to get very short of breath. Much longer and I was going to pass out. When I panted instead of answering, he sighed and released the spell. I tumbled to the tile, drawing in rasping breaths as I tried to get oxygen back into my body. I gave myself a two count and knowing he wasn't expecting it, I came up fighting. There's one thing I know about bullies, they might be tougher than you, they might hold most of the cards, but they don't like getting hit any more than anyone else and will turn their attentions elsewhere if they know bothering you will always mean a fight.

Just like with Teague and Edward Blake before him, I switched from magic to good old vanilla violence, my scything uppercut catching him just as he was about to speak. I followed it with a shot to his gut with my left hand. It bought me a second as he fell away from me which I used to then fling hastily summoned lightning into him. It blasted him back, taking him off his feet and tearing up the tile on the wall as it ripped through the air to find earth.

Tile showered down on him as he hit the floor. This was more like it: mess with me at your peril. I readied another spell, unconcerned about the damage I was doing, but Daniel wasn't staying down. I hit him with more lightning, but this time he deflected it, his right hand shooting out with the palm facing me. It arced away, smashing through two urinals which exploded in a shower of porcelain. Dust filled the air and water began shooting across the room to soak us both.

I pulled at the water, sending it directly at Daniel who once again deflected it, calling on elemental magic but keeping his demeanour visibly calm now that he was back on his feet. He made no effort to attack me and that was when I realised that he was letting me throw my worst at him so he could show me how pathetic it was.

I had a desire to try boiling his insides but as I felt the spell in my hand, I stopped myself from launching it. He would simply deflect that too. I was certain of it. Now that he had nothing to parry, he opened both his hands, one after the other, the right and then the left, letting each fall to his sides with the palms facing me. Then I watched the crackling red light of hellfire arcing and fizzing as it made its way down his arms to his hands, forming two red orbs.

'I can kill you without thinking, Otto,' he warned. 'Your ability with elemental magic is greater than any I have seen in over a hundred years. More powerful, I suspect, than Edward even. This is a good thing for me but if I have to bend you to my will, you will not enjoy it.'

The door to the gents' toilet burst open, a man in waiter's clothing coming through it. 'What's going on in here?' he demanded. Before he had the chance to even see anything, Daniel sent a ball of hellfire in his direction, blasting the man in the chest. It lifted him from the floor, flinging him against the wall in the corridor outside like a broken rag doll.

The door itself was ripped from its hinges leaving a large hole through which I could see how dead the man now was.

'That is what hellfire will do to you, Otto. Don't test me again.'

'Do you think I will help you capture and enslave people?' I snarled, desperate to restart the fight; certain knowledge of how that would go held me back.

Daniel tilted his head quizzically. 'Yes, Otto. Or I will kill you and then have free reign over Bremen. Events are unfolding that you cannot prevent. The human race will be enslaved, but it need not be a terrible thing. Once we return to Earth for good, we will stop the human race from destroying the planet as you have been. A few will die and a few will suffer but that is no worse than what you are doing to each other now.' I continued to stare at him with hate in my eyes. 'You gave me your word, wizard. That means something where I am from. If you wish, I can kill you now and take the girl as my familiar instead. She is young but I have time to train her.'

I could feel the need to fling spells at him. I had never performed an earth spell indoors before; certain it would bring the building down if I did. Perhaps now was the time to find out. Reaching out with my senses, I grasped more ley line energy and pushed tendrils of my thoughts into the ground, feeling it in my mind and making contact with the atoms there.

Approaching feet heralded another waiter, this one a woman, and Heike, coming to see where I had got to and probably guessing that the noise she could undoubtedly hear in the restaurant was being caused by me. The woman screamed upon seeing her fallen colleague and the burnt hole in his chest.

Daniel raised his hands, twin orbs of glowing red threat pointed at me and at Heike. Then he doused the one in his left, opened a portal and, with a wink, stepped backward through it to disappear. His voice drifted back, 'Make good choices, Otto.'

'We have to go,' I snapped at Heike, running forward through the spray of water.

'We can't,' she argued. 'We have to stay to deal with this. I'm a cop, and a man is dead.'

'Yes, Heike. He was killed by a demon. How do you plan to explain his injury? Daniel thought I was trying to run so he has sent the shilt back to Bremen, finding a way to renege on his promise already. If we don't get back there, they will tear through the town and it won't just be a werewolf we have to contend with.'

I wasn't hanging around to argue with her. My fatigue was gone; in its place was an uncontrollable desire to settle the score. At the end of the corridor with the dead waiter and the wailing waitress, I found a fire exit. It led outside to the street and back to the car, Heike trailing along as she tried to stop me.

'Otto, we can't just leave.' I kept going. She shouted at me, 'Otto, stop!'

I rounded on her, hopped up on adrenalin and too angry to hold myself back. 'Heike, you have no way of stopping me. Even if you were a cop right now, you couldn't arrest me because I wouldn't let you. I can't do anything for the man back there. I wish I could, but there are people about to get hurt in Bremen and I *can* help them. That's what I am going to do.' I was looming over her, looking dangerous and talking too loudly. It wasn't in her nature to cower away from me, but that's what she wanted to do. Her face, fear lurking at the edges even as she refused to show it, made me soften my stance and my voice. 'I could do with your help, Heike. The rules are changing. Let's save those who we can.'

There was no argument she could present that was going to work, no way for her to stop me, and she knew that I was right. 'I'll drive,' she said, holding out her hand for the keys. 'You drive like an old lady.'

Chapter 16

In the car on the way back, the fatigue started to creep over me again. I fought it, knowing that sleep now wouldn't do me any good. Instead, to keep myself awake, I focused on a very present problem, that of how to defeat the shifter.

While I did that, Heike called ahead to Klaus Nieswand. 'Klaus,' she cut in when he answered the phone. 'Have you had any reports of the shilt being spotted in Bremen or of anyone being attacked?'

'No,' he blurted. 'No. Didn't you say they weren't coming back because Daniel did a deal with Otto?' He sounded worried, scared even, like this was a personal nightmare coming back to haunt him. He was still shaken from his ordeal, not that it surprised me.

'We had a fight,' I told him.

'Who did?'

I went for the longer explanation. 'Daniel showed up in a restaurant in Magdeburg. He thought I was running from Bremen in a bid to escape him. We fought, mostly because I don't like bullies and he is punishing me for defying him by sending the shilt back to add to our problems.'

Heike cut in over me, 'You have to warn the guys on the ground. All the cops out patrolling need to treat this situation differently. They can't give the standard warning; it will just get them killed.'

Nieswand's voice came out as a croak. He stopped, gathered himself and tried again. 'They look like people here though, not the lizard looking things we saw over there. How will the cops know if it is a supernatural or a regular crazy person?'

It really was a good question. One to which neither Heike nor I could provide an answer. She said, 'Just make sure the chief knows, okay, Klaus?'

He said he would do whatever was necessary and disconnected.

Now that it was quiet in the car again, I went back to my werewolf problem. I imagined trying to take on Zachary because even if it wasn't him, it would be someone equally as dangerous and powerful.

In his transformed state, Zachary seemed invincible. I was sure that he wasn't, but he had taken a blast from Daniel's hellfire and stood back up. Daniel had been surprised but having seen what it did to the waiter in Magdeburg, I had to accept that Zachary was seriously tough. The simple assumption was that the same durability could be expected of any other werewolf I came across.

Back to the question then: how do I beat a creature like Zachary? In the open, I could use an earth spell provided we were in contact with the soil. It was arguably my most devastating spell in terms of massive effectiveness; in the immortal realm I used it to kill dozens of shilt in one go. What effect would that have on a werewolf I wondered and told myself it might not do much at all. He would just dig his way out again. Fire would burn, I was certain of that, it would inflict pain and most likely set fire to the coarse hair on his body. How would he react to a white-hot lance of fire? Would it drive him back or make him run straight at me to stop it? It wasn't a dumb animal I was dealing with after all. I went on like that for a while, performing spells in my imagination and running through the scenario of what it might do. Some looked more hopeful than others. Take an air spell for instance; for most it will pick them up and throw them about or will push them back or sideways or whatever I want it to do. It is a useful conjuring but the impact it would have on an enraged werewolf was limited. Limited to the point that I might as well just fart in its general direction and hope for the best.

'Everything okay over there?'

I turned to see Heike glancing at me, her attention split between the road and me. 'Yes. Why?'

'You looked like you were having an invisible fight with someone. Also, your eyes were closed, and your lips were moving.'

I hadn't realised. 'I'm trying to work out how to beat the werewolf when we meet it.'

'Coming up with much?'

'I guess I won't know until I try some things. I watched Zachary fight and he looked fairly hard to kill.'

Heike considered that for a while, her eyes on the road in front. We were past Hannover already, less than an hour from home. We were both hungry since dinner just hadn't happened, but there were more pressing issues. 'How's your cold?' she asked.

I had not thought about it for hours, that was the truth of it. Normally, when the symptoms of a winter cold come on, the fatigue and stiffness is quickly followed by a sore throat or a cough or a runny nose or all of them all at once. I had none of that. 'I don't think it is a cold. Not anymore. I think it's the other thing.'

'The demon blood thing?'

It seemed like an obvious conclusion to draw the moment they found the other blood inside me, but it genuinely felt more like a winter cold; why would demon blood, if that was what it was, cause winter cold-like symptoms? I didn't know what to make of it but there was one conclusion I could form. 'I don't feel as bad as I did.'

'No more split vision episodes?'

'Not since Daniel took Teague away last night.'

Heike pursed her lips and thought about it. 'This is good, right?'

I wanted to believe that. I wanted to have a second blood test so they could show me the weird extra blood was gone, but I worried they might show me it had taken over and my original blood was gone, replaced by whatever I got from Teague, if indeed that was where it came from. 'I don't know,' I concluded, worried what this process might do to me. Would I gain more magical ability? The portal thing would be good. If I could do that, I could still come back to visit Kerstin each night even after I went with Daniel.

'How about moonlight?' she asked.

'Huh?'

Heike repeated herself, 'How about using moonlight on the werewolf? Or sunlight? Whichever works.'

I shook my head, confused. 'I'm sorry, I'm not following.'

She tutted. 'You think it will be tough to fight the werewolf, right? So, can you force him to change back to human form? Would that make him easier to kill? Come on, wizard. You control the elements, right. Make the sun come up early.'

I burst out laughing. Yeah, I just rotate the entire planet super quick and catch the werewolf by surprise that way. I would probably cause a tidal wave that would kill every living thing on the planet right down to bacteria. When she glared at me for daring to laugh, I folded my bottom lip over my top one and thought about her suggestion. I mouthed the words silently, 'Change him back to human form.' The idea occurred to me when I first started to think about the problem but couldn't see how I would do it.

Was there something I could do with sunlight? Could I capture it somehow? It was an idea with merits. I leaned against the seat back to consider it. I don't remember falling asleep.

I woke up when Heike's phone rang. It came through on the car's speaker system, Schenk's annoying voice bringing me instantly alert.

'Thought you would just do whatever you wanted then?' he sneered down the phone at her. 'You're off the case, Dressler. You too Schneider. I don't want to see either of you again.'

Heike narrowed her eyes as she answered, trying to keep her voice calm and even, she said, 'You are being counterproductive, Schenk. We are tracking the missing girl and we...'

'I don't care what nonsense that idiot has filled your head with, Dressler. You should never have been promoted ahead of me and now I can reverse that. You know you only got the lieutenant's position because they needed to meet a demographic: so many women, so many ethnics, so many gay. Good luck with the hearing tomorrow.' Then he clicked off.

As Heike uttered some choice words, filling the car with expletives, her comment about the missing girl jolted me back to reality. I hadn't been looking at the compass. How long had I been asleep? Had I already missed her on the road?

I dug the compass from my pocket with a glance at Heike. Her knuckles were turning white on the steering wheel. 'That son of a bitch.' Heike made the comment through gritted teeth. 'He's been after my job for years, always trying to undermine me, always trying to make his mistakes my fault. I'm better qualified, more experienced and twice as bright.' I kept quiet while she ranted. I knew how she felt, everyone gets into a frustrating situation at some point. It's just part of life. While she spat fire in Schenk's name, I looked at the compass and conjured air to reactivate the tracking spell. It was still pointing ahead toward Bremen but now the signal was much stronger, no more than a few kilometres between us and wherever she was. Could she still be alive?

'He's going to get in early on my hearing,' snapped Heike, bringing my attention back into the car. 'They'll hear that he had to take me off the case because I'm unpredictable and cannot follow procedure; whatever bullshit he can find that will stick.' She caught herself in full rant mode and deflated with a quick glance at me. 'Sorry. None of this is your fault. He's just such an asshat. He would rather brown nose the chief and others than do any decent police work. We were both promoted to detective sergeant at the same time, but I got promoted to lieutenant when he was sure it should have been him and he's been a shit about it ever since.'

'I could make him explode?' I offered. I was mostly joking. She sniggered anyway. 'Lightning hits people all the time, you know?'

'That would be so great, Otto. Can you hit him in the butt? Make his fat ass explode?' She sniggered again, imagining him getting a lightning bolt in his ass.

The mirth was cut off by another phone call, the trill sound startling in the confines of the car. Heike glanced at the screen in the car's centre console where the number was displayed with the name Klaus Nieswand beneath it.

She thumbed a button on the steering wheel. 'Hi, Klaus.'

He immediately launched into an apology. 'Oh, God, Heike, I'm so sorry. That fat pig Schenk just announced that he had to take you both off the case. He heard me telling the chief what you told me about the shilt, and he went nuts. He had this big grin on his face when he found out you didn't get on the flight back from Brno. He was already aware that you were later to return than expected, but I had covered for you; I told him there was an accident by the airport and the traffic was moving slowly.'

'It's not your fault, Klaus,' she assured him. 'He would have found an excuse to make my life difficult no matter what.'

'I made it worse though,' he protested.

Dismissing his concerns, she asked, 'Have there been any attacks tonight?'

He blew out a breath which sounded defeated. 'Nothing at all. The chief paid attention when I told him an hour ago, even Schenk made sure to look concerned, but when the patrols all reported back that the streets were quiet, they all looked at me like I was sowing panic to cover up for you.'

Heike made a frustrated face. 'It's always quiet in the streets when it's this cold. Even the criminals stay home in the warm.'

'Won't that make it easier to respond if there is an attack?' I asked.

She nodded. 'Any chance Daniel was bluffing?' All I could do was shrug. She turned her attention back to Klaus. 'Look, Klaus, Schenk is an asshat, but you need to stay on the right side of him. Keep your head down and do what is expected of you.'

'Sure,' he said, 'I'm not sure what good that will do me; he sees me as in the same group as you two and therefore a problem to get rid of.' He sighed. 'I'll let you know if there are any developments.'

The phone clicked off just as we hit the offramp and left the autobahn. We were back in Bremen at least. 'What now?' asked Heike, glancing across the divide. 'Where do we go?'

'Head for the screams.' It was a flippant reply and unhelpful, so I quickly added, 'How about the station? Maybe we can appeal to Muller and get Shenk to back down a bit.'

She wrinkled her face in thought. 'I can't go running to daddy.'

'But *I* can beg him to see sense,' I argued. 'Schenk will let the supernaturals walk up and bite him on the ass before he acknowledges their existence. The chief has to see that we are trying to save lives; civilians and his officers.'

Heike hit her indicator, checked her mirror and threw the steering wheel around. I got that she agreed with my idea, but I wasn't sure the handbrake controlled one-hundred-and-eighty-degree turn was entirely necessary. I held on to the little handle thingy above my head as the car whipped around to face the other way, then found my kidneys pressed back into my seat as she powered in the other direction to a blare of horns.

'To the station,' she murmured, though I couldn't tell if she was happy about it or not.

Chapter 17

Heike's shouting drew the chief quickly enough. The desk sergeant had instruction to prevent her from entering the station. The instruction came from Chief Muller, he claimed, and she was going nuts, demanding that he be brought out to face her.

I had to agree with her sentiment; what the hell was he thinking? He knew we were trying to help. That was why he hired me in the first place. He hadn't issued the instruction to bar her entry though. When he lumbered into sight, I could tell by the perplexed look on his face that he had no idea why his presence was requested at the front desk.

'Where did the instruction come from?' he demanded of the desk sergeant, who, now that he was under the chief's gaze, looked a little crimson.

'Detective Sergeant Schenk passed it on,' he admitted guiltily, accepting that it had been a stupid order to enforce without first checking.

'Schenk?' the chief confirmed. The desk sergeant nodded obediently. 'Your drinking buddy, Schenk? That DS Schenk, yes?' Though I thought it impossible, the sergeant's flushed cheeks went a shade darker. Undoubtedly choosing to deal with the man later, Muller leaned forward to press the entry buzzer himself.

Heike wasted no time in shoving her way through the barrier and straight past the obstructive cop, never sparing him a glance. 'Are we off the case or not?' she asked.

'Schenk took you off the case?' The chief sounded genuinely surprised. Heike didn't bother to reply, her strides carrying her through the pit and out the other side to the corridor which contained the operations room. Muller called after her, 'He's not here.'

She slowed and stopped; her face clouded with questions. 'Where is he?'

'He put in seventeen hours already today. I sent him home. He has a wife and a child,' he pointed out, saying it gently, not berating her.

She got in his face anyway. 'Are you going to overrule him? This case needs Otto.'

The chief needed to take a step back because Heike was inside his personal space. He'd been around too long for that though. Instead, he calmly reached up, put three fingers on her chest where the top set of ribs meets the clavicles and pushed her back half a metre. 'Not yet. I will speak to him, but I assigned this investigation to him for a reason.'

'To replace me,' she snapped, instantly regretting it when she saw the hurt surprise on Muller's face. 'I'm sorry,' she said, lowering her voice. 'That wasn't fair.'

'No. It wasn't,' he agreed.

'Are any of the team here?' I asked, attempting to defuse the situation. 'We made a discovery in Prague and want to talk it through.'

'Moltz and Rugler are still working.'

We found them in the operations room with Eric Wengler, the profiler. It wasn't just them though. Voss was there again, plus two other men from the mysterious Supernatural Investigation Alliance who everyone else knew as the Kriminal Investigations Bureau. I still couldn't decide if these were good guys or bad guys; their military haircuts and outfits weren't doing them any favours on that front. To my mind it just aided the impression that they were itching to take over.

Three paces inside the room, Heike stopped as she looked all around. 'Where's Klaus?'

Rugler looked up from her computer. 'Schenk sent him home. He was here half of last night going over the evidence from Brno,' she added when Heike shot her a concerned look. Moltz nudged her with an elbow and she stopped talking.

He said, 'Sorry. We are under instruction to shut you out of the case and this room. Until you get reinstated...'

Heike waved him to silence. 'You don't have to explain. You do get that I outrank Shenk though, yes?'

Neither Rugler nor Moltz said a word, their expressions betraying that they weren't sure Heike would even be a cop after the hearing tomorrow.

'She stays,' insisted Voss, crossing the room. 'Both of them do.'

'You're not running the show here,' argued Moltz, no love lost between the two men.

Voss pierced Moltz with a mock hurt look. 'I can change that with a phone call. What do you think I will do about you when that happens?'

I got in between all of them. 'Enough!' I roared. 'There's no time for petty bickering.'

'Hey, we're just here to help,' Voss claimed.

'Are you?' I asked. 'What will you do if the werewolf is captured?'

'You are yet to prove that it is a werewolf,' he countered.

'Then why are there three of you here now when yesterday there was only one?' Heike asked.

'Simple prudence,' he replied, lying through his teeth. He believed it was a werewolf here, that I could tell. 'The attack at the Weber's house yesterday was most definitely supernatural, the killings witnessed last week were perpetrated by creatures we now know to be called shilt and Bremen *appears* to have a werewolf. It may prove to be something else, but this city has become a real hotspot for supernatural activity. Bliebtreu wants twice daily updates.' He turned to address me. 'As for your question. If we can, we will capture it.'

'Yes, how exactly did you take Zachary Barnabus captive?' I suddenly remembered that the reason I met him was because he was already incarcerated when they took me to their facility in Berlin. If they had a weapon or a method for capturing him, I wanted to know about it.

Voss looked unhappy when he admitted, 'He surrendered.'

I frowned at him. 'He surrendered?'

'He was surrounded and chose to not fight his way through all of us.' Finally, Voss said something true, admitting they were only able to take him because he opted to not kill them all.

It proved a point though. Turning to Heike, I said, 'This is what I mean about him. He is not the kind of person that rips other people apart.'

'You said it yourself, Otto. He might not be himself. If he got hit with the same juice as you, he might behave erratically. There's just no way to know.' I really wanted to argue but I knew it was my explanation she was using against me.

'What juice?' asked Voss.

I had no time for his questions though. 'Heike, I'm going to look for the girl; Zuzana. She's here in Bremen somewhere.'

'The missing girl from Brno?' Voss asked, his tone incredulous. 'You think she is here?'

'Yes, and she's our best lead yet.'

Heike interrupted, 'If she's alive.'

'Yes,' I agreed more quietly. 'If she's alive. I won't know until I find her.'

'How do you know she's here?' asked Moltz, getting up and taking an interest.

I took out the compass. 'You know I'm good at finding people, right?'

Everyone looked at the compass. The bubble of liquid was missing, the needle too, replaced by a small piece of wood from a barbecue skewer.

'It's a broken compass,' Voss pointed out then looked back up at me. 'Magic, right?'

'Yeah,' I replied, my patience already worn away. 'The girl, dead or alive, is in this city. I'm going out to find her.'

Voss immediately volunteered his men. 'Brubaker and Lange are going with you.'

I looked at the two men. Both were tall and well-built with very short hair and no trace of a smile. I wanted to argue that it might be too dangerous but just couldn't be bothered. They got a, 'Whatever,' as I started for the door. Before I got there, I turned around and walked backwards as I spoke to Heike, 'Go home, Heike. Get some rest and get ready for the hearing tomorrow. Maybe after that, you can take over here and we'll be a little more successful.' As I went through the door I shouted, 'I'll let you know when I find her.'

Chapter 18

I jogged out of the station, the two military-looking men easily keeping pace with me. I was moving quickly as I worried Heike would attempt to come with me. She had an important day ahead of her tomorrow and a family to see. Not only that, she could be of no use to me if we came across any shilt or indeed the werewolf. If Zuzana was alive, I expected her to be with him/it. Held captive for some reason I couldn't yet fathom.

'Where are we going?' demanded Lange as we hit the street and I turned right. I had no car, but in these conditions, I didn't really want to drive anyway. The trams were still operating, one gliding by at the end of the street ahead of us, and that was where I was going.

'You forget yourself,' I called over my shoulder. 'I have no use for you. This is likely to be dangerous. You should stay here.'

'We have our orders,' Brubaker replied, the pair of them jogging after me.

I hit the end of the road and swung myself around a lamppost. The tram was fifty metres ahead. An old lady was still getting off, a young woman helping her as she waited to get on. But we wouldn't get there before it pulled away again, the driver would spare no thought for people in the cold as he kept rigidly to his schedule. Lange and Brubaker both sprinted ahead to prove me wrong, getting on board and making sure the door couldn't close. No driver would ever move off with the doors open. Better to be slightly behind schedule than break health and safety protocol.

The tram would take us in the general direction of the town centre. Until I got closer, I wouldn't be able to pinpoint where the tracking spell wanted me to go. But now we were on the tram and I had a couple of minutes, I took a small tin from my pocket and started taking the small rings out of it, using a piece of sticking plaster to attach one between the second and third knuckles of each finger.

'What the hell are those?' asked Brubaker, unable to contain his curiosity.

I said, 'Protective amulets,' without looking up, quickly getting them all in place. In truth, I should keep them on all the time; they would have helped when Daniel turned up in Magdeburg. I couldn't predict when I might get attacked, so the only sensible thing was to always have them ready. They were ladies' rings though; little cameos or pretty gemstones and I felt a little self-conscious about them. I also found that I kept catching them on my clothing or in my pockets. There must be some trick to it that women learn at an early age, but I couldn't figure out. If I ever got five minutes, I was going to buy some that fit me and didn't make my hands look like they were trying to set a new fashion.

Getting the last one in place, I made two fists, mostly for my own confidence and checked the compass again. It was a good thing I did because the needle had swung through ninety degrees.

I jumped up, dinging the bell to let the driver know I wanted to get off but had to wait for him to reach the next marked stopping point. I dashed outside, forgetting to pay and drawing a shout of outrage from the conductor who raced after me. Lange grabbed his collar and wagged a finger in his face. The conductor wisely decided to let it go.

In the cold street, I had to orientate myself as I followed the compass. So much easier than using a flag as I had a few days ago, this method allowed me to keep going instead of constantly stopping to check direction. We were running along Violen Strasse, not far from the cathedral and heading toward the town hall. Normally, this part of town would be filled with tourists, getting out to see the sights even this late into the evening but the streets were deserted, the cold keeping everyone inside like Heike said.

However, that changed when we hit the corner near the cathedral. There were often homeless people in the plaza, drawn there by the abundance of tourists; lots of people meant more chance for spare change. It wasn't homeless people I was looking at now though, it was an army of shilt.

They were all facing our way, maybe more than a hundred, each with its short sword drawn and ready as if they had been waiting for me. None of them had bothered to disguise their features, the usual enchantments missing so Brubaker and Lange got the full effect. I heard them both gasp and pull their sidearms.

One stood apart from the rest at the front of the line, a leader perhaps. He lifted his sword arm and pointed it at me, a signal for the rest to charge, which they did. As one, they began running across the flagstone plaza, gathering speed.

'Get to safety,' I hissed, doubting either man would listen but not looking to see if they did. This looked and felt like an ambush, but I could find time for questions later. Right now, I needed to stay alive.

The shilt came as a solid wall, picking up speed. I wanted to use an earth spell, it would take out half of them or more in one hit, but I couldn't do that with a concrete base beneath the flagstones. I could feel it there when I reached out, so I hit them with air to disperse them, sending the right half flying as I funnelled air from my right hand. Then, as they faltered and tumbled from that, I hit the left half with a barrage of lightning, one blast after another. The blinding arcs tore into them, sending dozens skittering across the ground and killing many more.

I felt a brief sense of triumph; I was outmatching them easily, but just as I moved to close with them and pushed another air spell into my hand, I heard more feet behind me. A swift glance over my shoulder revealed at least as many shilt coming from the rear.

Now it had to be a deliberately sprung trap. They were coordinated and they had come with sufficient numbers to guarantee victory. Brubaker and Lange hadn't escaped, both men too brave, or too proud, to run away. They were firing into the mass of advancing shilt for all the good it did. The shilt looked confident, teeth showing in the streetlights as they continued toward us on all sides. The bullets were deflected each time, the short obsidian swords flashing out at impossible speed to knock them from the air. The only effect Brubaker and Lange had was when one shilt managed to deflect the bullet into the foot of the one next to him. I heard a howl and saw it tumble but there was no point in rejoicing their number reducing by one.

'Schneider!' yelled Lange as the shilt approached from two flanks. 'Schneider, what do we do?'

'Bullets don't have any effect!' yelled Brubaker, his voice betraying the faintest edge of panic.

Gritting my teeth, I snapped back. 'Not come with me. Stay on the tram. Run away when I told you to. Take your pick.' It pissed me off that I had to worry about them now. I had two hundred and something shilt to fight and I was hampered by having to protect these two idiots.

Looking around for something I could use, I spotted a large sycamore tree. I had no more than a few seconds and a hastily contrived plan. There was an abundance of ley line energy here, there always was near churches and religious sites no matter what the denomination of the religion was. Perhaps the lines shifted, drawn here by the flock of people worshipping, or maybe the churches picked the spots because of all the Earth's energy gathering there. I doubted I would ever know, but it meant I had a limitless supply to pull through me now as I pushed my senses into the tree. No one on the city council would thank me for this, but as I focused on the molecules of water inside the tree and began to pull them to me, I shouted to the men behind me. They were still firing pointlessly at the shilt making it difficult for them to hear me. Mercifully, they paused when they could hear that I was trying to tell them something.

'I'm going to make a gap. You need to get through it and don't look back. Just run and get to safety.'

Then I yanked on the tree with all my might, simultaneously pouring an earth spell into the soil around its roots to loosen them. As it came free, I switched to an air spell to guide where it fell and push it away from me. It fell to the right as I flung the entire tree across the plaza toward one advancing flank of shilt. It had to have killed twenty of them as it landed, and it skidded twenty metres to take out a load more. Instantly, it created a channel.

Dropping the spell, I slapped Lange on his shoulder and screamed, 'Run,' in his ear. The shilt were almost upon us, seeing the destruction I had wrought and wanting to get in tight for close quarter fighting where they might stand a better chance. A shockwave of air cleared the route for Brubaker and Lange, but I could do no more for them because I was about to get skewered by dozens of black swords.

I cursed my bravery which had spurred me to valour when I probably should have focused on saving myself but did the one thing I believed would save me: I flew.

I'm still calling it flying, even though I could hear a cartoon space man telling me it was falling with style. The first pulse of air drove me upwards, out of the reach of the shilt just before they got to me. Up was only going to bring me right back down on top of them though just as dozens of very sharp-looking swords were pointing up at me, so I pushed more air to drive myself toward the cathedral. If I could get over the top of them and land with the cathedral behind me, I would have them all facing me on one flank. A wide flank maybe, but a single flank, nevertheless.

I suck at flying though.

The second blast of air didn't have enough down in it, so I shot toward the cathedral, but my trajectory was off, and I was going to slam into an army of shilt where I would get hacked to pieces. I couldn't switch to a spell like fire or lightning to scatter them because then I wouldn't be flying at all and would just impact the ground from ten metres up.

I corrected before I crashed into them, overdid it and flew right back over where I started from. Each blast downward scattered more of the enemy below, but they soon got wise and started to throw their swords at me. Suddenly the air was filled with flying shards of obsidian, scaring me into flying even higher to evade them. If I lost control now, I wouldn't have to worry about the shilt, I would do the job of killing myself for them.

One advantage came from being too high up for their swords to reach me; I could see Brubaker and Lange had made it to safety. The shilt weren't interested in them and hadn't pursued their escape. They were both across the far side of Am Dom, the wide road running in front of the cathedral where they were now watching me flailing about in the air.

I told myself to breathe and keep calm, panic would serve no purpose. The shilt were following me like a tennis crowd, their heads tracking my movement above them. My aiming mark was still the cathedral, but I allowed myself to drift further toward the road, drawing them in that direction so I had a bigger gap behind them in which to attempt a landing.

Clamping my teeth together so I wouldn't bite my tongue in half when I stacked my landing, I went for it, zipping over their heads in a downward trajectory as I conjured air to push myself forward with a touch of down pressure so I wouldn't just plummet. Angling the spell to create a cushion of air when I got within a few metres of the ground, I touched down as lightly as if I had stepped off an escalator. It made me wish there were more people watching.

I couldn't help but smile at myself, my newly discovered skill one I would have to put to good use and practice with when I got the chance. The smile didn't last though as the banshee cry of the shilt running at me drew my attention back to the very real possibility that I was still about to get killed.

It was lucky for me that the shilt seem to be the foot soldiers of the immortal realm. Had they been supported by another wizard like Edward, or worse, a demon like Daniel, I wouldn't have lasted more than a few seconds. As it was, I was unscathed so far but there were so many of them there was nothing in my arsenal that could take them out all at once.

I had created a twenty-metre gap which would equate to four seconds, if that. My back was pressed to the wall of the cathedral as I let rip with lightning. Fire was no good; it was deadly, but too focused. I had never worked out how to engulf a large area with it, but as I thought that, an insane idea formed in my head.

I could grasp individual molecules of water and I could grasp individual molecules of soil. I could also push heat into either if I so chose. But what could I do with stone? I had never tried it before. Not once in my entire life had I attempted to heat a stone with magic. I had to wonder if the shilt had picked this spot for the ambush deliberately because there was no earth for me to conjure. They had seen the effect of my earth spell a few days ago.

It was time to find out what I could do. Buying time by whipping a tornado into shape and unleashing it into them from behind, I distracted most of the advancing wall of shilt, but it wasn't going to slow them down for long. The few at the front got treated to a blast of fire to stop them from getting to me, but then I switched my effort, feeling out into the flagstones and the concrete beneath it.

Despite the cold air biting at my face, I could feel sweat forming on my brow. The effort of conjuring so much magic, combined with stark terror was pushing my own body temperature up. It was a struggle, to grasp enough of the stone for what I needed to do but I could feel it changing as my spell took hold. Pulling ley line energy through me at an unprecedented rate, my right hand began to feel hot and then began to feel like it too was burning. I closed my eyes, telling myself I either pulled this off or they were going to kill me anyway. I couldn't run to save myself. Or fly for that matter. To do so would turn a small army of bloodthirsty shilt loose on the city. I had to stand my ground and take them here.

Knowing any second could be my last, I kept my eyes shut, panting from the effort and ignoring the pain in my hand, and then it happened. The screams told me I had done it.

My eyes snapped open. Just in time to see a black sword coming my way, thrown from the crowd as they all burst into flame. I ducked under it, feeling its passage move my hair but it couldn't detract from what I had done. About a fifty-metre diameter chunk of the stone plaza had changed state from solid to liquid, the concrete beneath it too.

I had created lava!

The shilt were trapped, their feet sinking into the molten stone as the heat from it set their clothes alight to consume them. I had utterly destroyed a Bremen landmark that had stood for a century or more and ripped up a tree that had to be older than me. It was all repairable.

Feeling victorious, I screamed at them, 'Ha! How'd you like a volcano up your butt?' Too carried away, I failed to see the shilt at the far right of the dying mass. He made it through the morass of molten stone, emerging on fire and demented with pain. I didn't see it because it just looked like more fire, until he threw his sword.

From the corner of my eye, the movement made me flinch and I turned to face the danger. Too late though as the sword beat my spell casting, impaling my right shoulder with a sickening strike that bowled me off my feet. As I tumbled backward, screaming in pain as heat from the sword sizzled on my flesh, the maddened shilt advanced, snatching up a sword from the floor. He was going to end me right now. I had killed an army in one go, only to lose to the last dying effort of a single soldier.

I raised my right arm, trying to push a spell into it even through the pain, but I couldn't lift it and I couldn't get my hand to work. He was still coming. I had time to beat him if I could just create a spell, but when I glanced at my right hand, I saw that it too was burnt. Red and blistered from the effort pushed through it. Cursing myself, I let my head flop back.

There was no more fight in me.

The shilt couldn't have been more than two seconds from driving the sword through my chest, but after four seconds he still hadn't arrived, so I took my eyes off the peaceful stars I was staring at to glance down the length of my body and through the gap between my feet. There I found a familiar face standing over me with the dead shilt hanging from one hand.

'Need me to bail you out again, wizard? I know I've said it before, but you are such a disappointment.'

Chapter 19

Zachary Barnabus dropped the dead shilt. 'Are you doing okay there, wizard? You don't look so good.'

'Really?' I managed, making my response sound sarcastic and looking at him as I spoke. I couldn't hold my head up for long though, relaxing again to let the back of it rest against the mercifully cold stone. Zachary Barnabus was here. He had just saved my life and it wasn't for the first time. He always looked casual and nonchalant about everything going on and always had a clever line to deploy at the right moment. I glanced at him again. It was well below freezing and he was wearing a white t-shirt, jeans and a pair of workman's boots. He didn't even look cold. His boyband good looks were complimented by a daft hairstyle that was too long on top but appeared to be styled that way deliberately.

'Here let me give you a hand,' he said. He didn't mean a hand to get me up though, he grabbed the hilt of the short sword sticking out of the meaty part of my right shoulder and yanked it free in one go.

I screamed for all I was worth and called him some choice and, dare I say it, quite inventive names.

'That's the spirit,' he laughed. 'Feel better now?'

'Feel better?' I asked incredulously. 'Zachary, if I could wield a spell right now, I would stick a lightning bolt right up your arse.'

He gave me a sideways look. 'You want to stick something up my arse? I always wondered about you.'

In the three days since I last saw him, I had forgotten what a snarky dickhead he was.

'Are you finished with these guys?' he asked, indicating the shilt. The stone hadn't stayed molten for long. The moment I stopped pouring energy into it, the cold air set it again so now it looked like a puddle with lumps in it. I could make out burnt bodies poking through the surface here and there. It was horrendous to think that I had done that. 'Only, I arrived too late and you had done for them all and I feel like I missed out on all the fun. There's a couple I trapped under a rock around the corner just in case you needed to open a portal or something. I remember what a douche you were last time because I killed too many of the things that were trying to kill us.'

He waited for me for to answer but I was looking at my blistered right hand and wondering how many months it would take to heal back to a useable state. The burns looked deep which would mean it might never work the same again.

'Hello, Earth to wizard.' I looked up at Zachary. 'Do you need the ones I saved? If not, I'll just pop off and kill them now.' He made like he was turning to go.

'No, wait. I think we need to send them back. They can carry a message.'

'Can't I just kill one of them?' he whined.

Seemingly from out of nowhere, something hit him in the chest. It caught him off guard and made him stumble back a pace in surprise. Then he was hit again, also on the chest but slightly higher, so it was nearer his neck than his nipples. They were taser wires.

I could see smoke coming off them, little sparks flickering where they had gone through his t-shirt, because that was all he had on his top half, and into his skin.

He looked down at them, looked up and along the wires to where they had come from and tore them out with his right hand in one motion. I tracked their trajectory also, finding, as expected, Brubaker and Lange staring at him in surprise. They saw him move and both went for their sidearms since the tasers hadn't worked.

I swung myself up and onto my feet, getting into Zachary's way as he started toward them. The light in his eyes was already changing, a bright red glow starting to form behind his irises. I shouted, 'Everyone, stop!' which was about all I had the energy for. I then proved how beaten I was by collapsing. I honestly thought Zachary would catch me and that would distract him from killing the two Alliance guys. But the big werewolf, currently in human form, just watched me fall, looking down at me with a single raised eyebrow as he shook his head in a clear display of disappointment.

Brubaker shouted, 'Get down on your knees!' as he pointed his weapon at Zachary. Meantime, Lange was stepping to his right so the pair of them were not so close they made a single target.

Staring down to me at his feet, Zachary asked, 'Are these two idiots with you?'

I swivelled myself around to face Brubaker and Lange. 'Guys put the weapons away.'

Lange was on his radio though, calling for back up, 'We have the beast. I repeat; Barnabus is here. We have him cornered.'

Zachary looked around to see just where the corner he was supposed to be cornered in was.

'Get on your knees and interlock your hands behind your head,' Brubaker ordered again.

Zachary looked down at me once more. 'I'm going to get bored and hurt them in a minute, wizard. This is why I steer clear of cities. Too many people who are altogether too stupid.'

'This is your last chance,' Brubaker warned. Lange was off the radio and had both hands back on his gun. They looked confident but nervous. They had the number one suspect in their sights and would shoot him if they had to. Either way they would come out of it looking like heroes and taking him down would tend to their bruised egos after I made them run from the shilt army.

Zachary growled at them. 'No, this is *your* last chance.'

'They think you killed a bunch of people,' I blurted. 'You need to give yourself up so we can clear your name and focus effort on catching the real killer.'

Tired of waiting, Brubaker opened fire. The single shot echoed loudly in the still night air. It was designed as a warning shot. A final, final warning if you will. It went wide, intentionally missing its target, but Zachary exploded into action anyway.

Moving so fast it didn't look possible, especially for a man his size, he closed the distance to Brubaker before he could get another shot off, ducking under his aim to pop up again with a blow to Brubaker's midriff that lifted him off the ground and had to have caused internal damage. His gun went skittering across the stone as he flew backward. He would have landed several metres away in a heap, but Zachary snagged his left leg out of the air. Whipping him around, he used his own momentum to turn Brubaker into both a shield and weapon. Flinging him like a rock, he sent the man flying toward Lange, his unconscious body covering ten metres in a heartbeat and without once touching the floor. Lange didn't stand a chance, there was nowhere he could go that would get him out of the way of the flailing limbs, so he caught his partner full in the chest, the pair of them ending up on the flagstones.

Zachary's rage was up now, and he was moving in to finish the job. Sensing that I had no choice if I wanted to save them, I managed to lift my right arm despite the agonising pain from my shoulder. I shouted a warning, but Zachary wasn't listening. He was too mad to hear me, so I blasted him with a bolt of lightning.

It hit him square in his right ear. The effect was a lot like throwing a stone at an elephant for all the damage it did. It got his attention though, the giant man turning his head my way.

'You want something, wizard?' he growled.

'Yes, actually. I want you to not kill either of those men. It would cause complications.'

'I wasn't going to kill them,' he protested as if that should have been obvious. He bent down and took Lange's weapon, checked him over for any other weapons, took extra magazines and tucked the lot into his pockets. 'I don't kill people,' he said as he straightened up.

'Then it isn't you that has been killing pimps and strip bar owners across Europe?' I asked hopefully.

'What? No, wizard, it isn't me. I think whoever it is discovered their ability recently. It came to me in my teens and it was very difficult to control at first. I came back to find out if that is what this is and to help. I was having a nice quiet time in the country and then I go into a bar and my face is all over the damned television. Who do I have to thank for the Europe-wide man hunt?' He stopped talking so I could answer, but then he was looking at me critically, tilting his head as he inspected me. 'Weren't you dying a moment ago?'

'Huh?' He was right. Zachary pulled a sword from my shoulder a few minutes ago. How was it that I wasn't bleeding to death? I held up my right hand. 'It's healing,' I whispered in awe.

I rolled my right shoulder to test it, got hit with a burst of pain and almost collapsed. As my legs went out and I had to duck my head from a severe case of the whirlies, Zachary grabbed the back of my jacket, keeping me upright.

'You suck, wizard. A tiny little scratch and you go all floppy.'

'I had a sword through me,' I argued. I felt I had a valid point. I had to see the wound though because I ought to be in far worse condition than I was and feel far worse than I did. Using my left hand, I forced the poppers on my coat open and yanked the zip down. I was cack-handed but I got it open and then had to wriggle around as I tried to pull my sweater away from my chest so I could look down inside my shirt.

Zachary got bored waiting for me to manage by myself. 'Here,' he offered, sticking his hands out and beckoning that I turn toward him. When thoughtlessly I did, he grabbed a chunk of sweater and shirt in each hand and ripped them apart. The sweater ripped down the middle, my shirt just ripped open as all the buttons popped off.

'Thanks,' I said, not meaning a word of it. The sweater had been a gift from my wife.

'You're very welcome,' he replied with a small bow.

Now that I had complete access to my chest, I could ease the shirt back to look at where the blade had gone in. I had a terrible cut, a deep hole at least fifteen centimetres long and it was gaping half a centimetre open in the middle. It had bled but it was barely bleeding now. Like my hand, it was already healing.

Zachary was looking at it too. 'Is that normal?' he asked, his brow knitted in question.

'Not even nearly.' I thought about what this might mean, and a question surfaced. 'When I exploded Teague the other night, I got a burst of magical energy from him and covered in atomised demon. It has changed something inside me, I think. You got hit with the same thing. Have you been feeling ill the last few days?'

'I've never felt ill in my entire life.' I eyed him sideways. 'Really. Colds, flu, sore throat, all that stuff. I've never had any of them. I got inoculations as a kid, long before all the shifter stuff started happening to me, but I don't remember ever being ill as a kid either.'

I wanted to explore what effect Teague's blast of energy might have had on him just as I wanted to know more about what was happening to me, but we both needed to get out of here. Lange's call for backup would result in the Alliance descending on us soon enough, if not the police as well. Then I remembered why I had left the station in the first place. Cursing myself, I pulled the compass from my pocket, glad it was on my left side, so I didn't have to use my damaged right hand. Zachary saw it in my hand. 'You know that's broken, right, wizard? Is it magical?'

'Only sort of. I use it for tracking spells like when we found Heike at the barn. This is just better than the piece of bunting I used then.' I called forth air to guide the needle, got my direction again and started to move. I was injured, badly injured in fact with the cut to my shoulder and the burnt hand, but it just didn't seem to be bothering me that much. I had just killed an army of shilt, now was the time to rescue a girl, and then see if I had any superhero capes since I could fly now.

'Who are you trying to find this time?'

'A missing girl. She might be dead, she might be alive. I won't know until I find her, but I tracked her here from Brno.'

'Czech Republic?'

'Yup.'

'On foot?'

I scrunched up my face. 'No, dummy. I drove. She's close, so I'm going to find her now.'

'Wizard,' called Zachary as I walked away. When I looked back at him, he said, 'The two shilt I trapped in case you needed to do anything with them. Do I get to kill them now?'

'I thought you didn't kill people.'

'They're not people, wizard. They're... actually I don't know what to classify them as, but no one cares if I kill them so...' He motioned over his shoulder with both hands. He was just going to quickly dispatch them before we set off.

I called after him, 'Wait.' He paused, wanting to see why I stopped him. 'I have an idea.'

Chapter 20

The shilt were exactly where he had left them. When he said under a rock, I figured it was a metaphor, but no, they were under a boulder. It was part of a feature garden in the grounds of the cathedral and looked to weigh several hundred kilos. Too heavy for the shilt it seemed as one of them was dead already; crushed by the weight. The other had managed to survive but wasn't looking too chipper now that the rock was no longer on him.

'Are you going to die?' I asked it.

'You tell me,' he winced, wanting to fight, but having no fight left in him.

'No, what I mean is; are you so badly hurt that you are going to die anyway? I need you to carry a message for me.'

He gave me a doubtful sideways look, expecting there to be a catch or something. When I had nothing to add, he said, 'Okay.'

For emphasis I grabbed his collar and pulled his face closer to mine. 'When you get back to the immortal realm, you tell your little shilt friends and anyone else who thinks coming to Bremen to prey on the humans is a good idea, that Bremen has a defender.'

Zachary rolled his eyes. 'Oh, boy.'

Ignoring him, I pressed on, 'Anyone coming here, demon, shilt or otherwise, is going to get a face full of hurt. You are the last survivor from tonight's excursion. You go back and tell them to go someplace else. If they come here, I will find them, and I will kill them.'

'You can't kill the demons,' he argued, 'Why do you think we are so subservient to them. We have to do what they say.'

'Wait a second.' I glanced at Zachary, but he wasn't paying any attention. 'Are you telling me your little army was sent here by a demon tonight?' He nodded glumly. Daniel said he unleashed them, but this was an ambush. Had he changed his mind about taking me as his familiar?'

'What was your instruction? Were you sent here just to kill me?' I was right in his face now, anger boiling up and threatening to spill over.

'No. We were to catch you and bring you back. Then we could return to Bremen and do whatever we wanted.' The shilt was eyeing Zachary and me nervously, convinced one of us was about to kill him.

I let go of his jacket, some of the burnt skin from my right hand sticking to the fabric though I barely noticed. 'Why would Daniel order my capture?' I asked myself. 'He could have taken me himself a few hours ago.'

Despite the hushed manner in which I had spoken, the shilt heard me. 'It wasn't Daniel.' I shifted my eyes to look at his in question. 'Daniel didn't send us,' he repeated.

'So, who did?'

He looked about nervously, not wanting to say but not feeling that he had a choice. As he opened his mouth to speak, a bolt of red energy shot from behind us. The shilt's eyes had just enough time to widen in terror before the hellfire blast hit it in the chest and killed it instantly just as it had the waiter in Magdeburg.

Zachary and I went straight into defensive mode, turning and darting. Zachary began to transform as he ducked behind the rock, tearing at his clothes to get them off. From the corner of my eye, I noticed the shilt had been blasted backwards, but where I expected him to now be lying, his body was crumbling to dust and blowing away on the breeze. I had no time to dwell on it, and pulled up a defensive barrier, hoping it would keep me alive long enough to find better cover or maybe escape. We really needed to vacate the area before the authorities or the Alliance turned up, but as I brought my head around to see who I now faced, I had to gasp in shock.

The tallest person I had ever seen was standing twenty metres away. He was hugely muscled and over two and a half metres tall. To his left and right, he was flanked by thirty figures. Male and female, they ranged in size and build, but none were anywhere near as terrifying as the one in the middle and every last one of them was a demon.

'I sent them,' the tall figure said. Fully transformed, Zachary came out from behind the rock looking dangerous and ready, but there was nothing we could do against a platoon of demons. 'Ah, the shifter too. How very convenient.'

'Who are you?' I demanded, wanting to know the name of the creature about to end my life.

With a smile, he said, 'I am Beelzebub, ruler of the place you recently visited without invitation. You made a bit of a mess. So much so in fact, I thought we should have a conversation. When one of the shilt I sent returned a few minutes ago claiming you had wiped them all out, I killed him for lying. It was only my advisor Nathaniel who convinced me that we ought to investigate. So, here we are. What a nasty little place it is. I shall have to appoint someone I don't like to rule this region when we all return.'

There was an exchange of words as one of the demons closest to him said something we couldn't hear. Beelzebub leaned his head down slightly, then nodded and turned his attention back to me.

'Nathaniel tells me you are bound to Daniel, is that correct?'

I answered with a nod.

He appeared to consider it for a second. 'That is the only thing keeping you alive. I shall be watching though. Your master has been of use but his unquenchable desire for power concerns me. If you do not prove to be of use to our cause, your demise will have only been delayed.'

Zachary chose to interrupt him, 'You say your name is Beelzebub? Shouldn't you have horns?'

The giant demon turned his head and eyes slowly through a few degrees to look his way. 'That's just common human nonsense. You invented the concept of religion and created a beast that would punish you for your sins. Well, I guess you got some of that right because you have ruined this planet and I will be back soon to rule it. When I do, the humans will suffer for what they have done.'

'You ought to have gone with the horns. It would help with your image.' I was getting to know what Zachary was like and I doubted he was about to do our cause any good. I was right, of course, because the next thing he said was, 'You might want to consider a complete makeover, in fact, because right now you look like a giant dickhead.'

Beelzebub raised a single eyebrow. 'What an odd character you are.' Then he shot a single orb of hellfire from his right hand. I darted forward to get my barrier in the way, protecting the werewolf from his own stupid mouth. The blast of dark red energy diffused against the barrier, destroying it instantly.

I whispered, 'Dancer,' to bring up the next barrier, counting off nine in my head. Each bolt of hellfire would take out a barrier and I only had ten of them. They would be gone in seconds if all the demons started shooting. I didn't see a way out.

'Are you still using reindeer names for your spells, wizard?'

'They're easy to remember,' I replied defensively.

He tutted as he started to move away from me, turning his back on the demons so he could look at me when he said, 'You are such a disappointment.' Then he spun back around to face the demons and clapped his hands together. 'How about it then, big man? You and me. Tell your knob jockeys to holster their weapons and let's see which of us is actually tough.'

His request raised a lot of eyebrows and drew sniggers from his opponents.

No one got to hear Beelzebub's answer though because all the demons turned to face a fresh threat. Balls of red death appeared in every set of hands as across the plaza, a new force arrived through half a dozen portals. I had enough time to wonder what fresh hell we now faced, about a millisecond in total, before the demons started firing. If they hadn't, I would have assumed it was yet more demons come to ensure Zachary and I had no means of escape, but when the new arrivals began to return fire, the orbs they formed were not dark red, but a light blue.

There were dozens of them, a far greater force than Beelzebub had but he gave no ground, roaring for his troops to, 'Repel them!'

For a moment I found myself transfixed by the spectacle, but Zachary yanked me to the ground and behind the rock. 'Who'd you think this new bunch is?' he asked, calm as anything.

The answer was obvious. They were the opposing force to the demons. 'They're angels.'

Even in werewolf form, Zachary could raise one eyebrow. 'Like with harps and wings and shit?'

'I think that's the point,' I replied. 'They don't have any of that. They never did. They probably don't call themselves angels and demons either. Like Beelzebub said, "We invented religion." I think we came up with names for the things we remembered. Humanity remembers them as those on the side of the humans and those who would enslave us. Angels and demons.'

'You know, wizard? I can never tell when you are talking crap or not. It's quite a skill.'

I peeked around the rock. The two forces were blasting the hell out of each other, figures getting hit and toppling, but others catching the incoming fire to diffuse it and then returning it with interest. Those who were hit, didn't stay down, immortality making the fight pointless in many ways.

I nudged Zachary. 'Come on, we have to go.' The missing girl was still out there, distractions from shilt and demon had already delayed me long enough.

'Dammit,' Zachary swore behind me.

'What?'

'I can't get to my clothes.' I just gave him a look. We had bigger issues than losing a favourite pair of trousers. Seeing my face, he said, 'Have you any idea how hard it is to find clothes in my manly proportions? It's alright for tiny men like you.'

'Poor baby,' I shot back and ran for some nearby bushes. We would have to take the long way around, but it was a much better idea than staying where we were.

Chapter 21

We ran for more than a hundred metres, getting some distance between us and the battle ensuing outside the cathedral. Whoever was responsible for the grounds and the plaza was going to have a hell of a clean-up job tomorrow. Not only that, the blasts that weren't finding their target were hitting the cathedral itself, knocking chunks out of it and smashing windows.

Once safely away from the melee, I slowed my pace and took out the compass again. Holding it in my right hand, I saw that the skin was continuing to heal. I wiggled my fingers, which caused some discomfort as the scabs cracked and split in several places. This was a minor inconvenience as it was undeniably healing. I shouldn't have been able to use it. Ever.

This wasn't the time to dwell on it. The compass swung, giving me a direction, but as I looked up to see where it was pointing me, I realised it wasn't the same direction it had been telling me to go earlier. That meant just one thing: she was moving. I got excited just for a heartbeat before reminding myself that it could be her killer moving her body around in the boot of a car like the couple in Prague.

Sirens reached my ears; they were distant but approaching and it sounded like a lot of them. 'The cops are coming,' I commented as I got up.

'Are you only just hearing that?' asked Zachary.

'Yes. Why? How long ago did you hear them?'

'Five minutes ago, maybe. Before the demons showed up anyway.'

Werewolf hearing was something else. 'Come on, she's this way,' I beckoned as I started across the road. He kept to the shadows as much as he could. It was late evening now, past bedtime for a lot of people and the cold was keeping the streets empty. A huge werewolf is quite conspicuous though and there were still cars out on the roads.

The compass led us away from the cathedral, heading for the park and the windmill café that dominated it. Once we crossed Am Wall, we came out of the old part of the city, and with the park in front of us, there was nowhere for a car to be. My hope that Zuzana might still be alive picked up.

As we hit the grass, still following my tracking spell, I saw that I was right to have hoped.

I was also massively wrong.

Zachary flexed his huge arms, extending his knife-like claws so they caught the moonlight in the frigid air. Our breaths were coming out as clouds as we both huffed from our exertion, and there, just ahead of us, was the werewolf and my compass was pointing straight at it. Zuzana hadn't been killed by the beast, nor had she been taken by it and dragged here. Zuzana was the werewolf, and she had just killed again.

In her transformed state, she wasn't as tall as Zachary, nor as muscular, but she was still enormous and utterly terrifying to look at. There was nothing friendly or inviting about her features. Unlike a dog, who is super cute as a puppy, but still endearing as a mature animal, werewolves emit a vibe that screams death and horror. Zuzana was no exception.

Hanging from her right hand was a man. He wasn't dead. Not yet, at least and I couldn't see any injuries on him, but he wasn't trying to get away even though I could see his hands moving weakly. I didn't know who he was, but I intended to save him.

The three of us were doing nothing but staring at each other, Zuzana's shoulders rising and settling with her breathing, but she made no other movement as she assessed us. In the quiet of the park, the sound of approaching sirens echoed out from between the buildings.

Zachary spoke, 'My name is Zachary. We are not here to hurt you.'

Her features were hard to read, but to me she looked more annoyed than anything else. In response to his opener, she looked down at the man hanging from her hand. He groaned a little and tried to lift his head. When she looked back up, she said, 'Who's your pet?'

She was talking about me. Not that I took offense. This had to be a terribly confusing time for the young woman, but she had killed a bunch of people and needed to be stopped. I couldn't see a way out of this for her that didn't end with incarceration.

I lifted my arms, activated a barrier by saying, 'Prancer,' and readied an earth spell. My best bet was to disable her. I knew what limited effect lightning, fire, and everything else had on Zachary, so I had to go bigger. Normally that would mean trying to blow her up from the inside, but I genuinely didn't want to hurt her.

The sirens continued to get closer.

'You need to surrender,' I stated as confidently as I could. 'We will stop you if we have to, but the killing stops now.'

She laughed. 'Surrender? Why ever would I do that? I finally found some freedom.'

I pushed my senses into the earth around her. I wanted to open it up right under her feet and drop her in, but I didn't want to bury her, just get enough of her in so that she couldn't effectively fight back.

Zachary took a step toward her. 'It doesn't have to be like this. Your life doesn't have to be like this. Come with me, Zuzana. Let me take you to safety.'

She frowned at him, caught off guard because he knew who she was. 'How do you know my name?'

I answered first. 'I tracked you here, from Brno, Zuzana.' I could feel the earth, it was frozen solid and would be hard to move in the way that I wanted to, so I began to heat it, just enough to melt the ice crystals inside it. I didn't want to rip a hole in the ground underneath her and have it come away in one giant lump. 'You killed your uncle, didn't you? Was he abusive, Zuzana?'

It was the wrong thing to ask.

With a scream of defiance, she thrust her left hand down at the chest of the man she held, driving her talons into it. He gasped and gagged. There was nothing I could do to help him, I just hadn't been fast enough, but this had to end here, so with an almighty yank on the earth, I ripped a chunk of it free.

The heat energy I pushed into the water hadn't had enough time to work, so it really was a chunk that tore out of the ground; two metres across and a metre deep in a ragged circle with Zuzana the werewolf standing right on top of it. I wanted to upend the earth outwards so she would fall into it, but I had the opposite effect, lifting her into the air so she was thrown sideways.

Tumbling, she growled and dropped the man, his ruined body falling to the frozen ground to land in the hard-packed snow. The spell hadn't worked at all and I wouldn't have the chance to use another earth spell any time soon. All I had really done was shown my hand early. Now she was rolling with the momentum and bouncing back onto her feet. When she stood up, she looked mad.

A guttural growl escaped her lips as she came up into a ready pose. Her arms were out to each side, claws extended, and boy did they look deadly. 'What are you?' she hissed.

Zachary got in first. 'He's some kind of magician or something. He's real fun at parties.' Always the joker, he got serious for a second. 'I meant what I said, Zuzana. We are not going to hurt you, but you must come with me now. It's that or the police. You won't be able to evade them forever and you have to stop killing people.'

'The police? They couldn't stop me if they tried,' she scoffed, and she was probably right. 'I don't know you and I certainly don't trust you just because you can shift like me. Why don't you come with me instead?'

She was circling us, moving back toward the old part of the city, but before Zachary could say anything else, the sirens doubled in volume as they burst onto Am Wall and began tearing along it in our direction. They probably weren't coming for us; they would be responding to reports of events at the Cathedral, but they saw us anyway.

We were a frozen Tableau; the three of us in a standoff we had failed to negotiate when the cars caught sight of us. The moment we were spotted was obvious, because all three cars locked up their wheels at the same time. The road was mostly free of ice and snow, the gritters having done their job, but it was the face staring out at me from the front passenger seat that caught my attention. Schenk saw Zachary and Zuzana, but it was me he was jabbing his finger at.

Zuzana turned, taking off like an Olympic sprinter as her powerful legs bit into the ground to propel her forward. Zachary went after her, also eating up the ground faster than could be believed. An air spell, hastily concocted to push a wall of air in her way had almost no effect at all, causing her to stumble a pace as she hit it and kept going. Then they were across the road and gone, running between the buildings to vanish. Two of the squad cars chased them though I was certain they wouldn't catch sight of them again.

I turned to face Schenk as he struggled to get his oversized body out of the low seat. 'Schneider!' he screamed at me. 'I knew it. I just knew it.'

'What?' I shouted back as he lumbered toward me, a young uniformed cop hot on his heels, his weapon drawn and held low but ready.

'You're with them. Place him under arrest,' he snapped at the uniform. He hadn't even looked in the direction of the retreating werewolves, his interest in them zero because all he wanted was me.

I backed up a pace and squinted at the fool. 'You're an idiot, Schenk. I just identified the werewolf; it's the girl from Brno, the one who went missing. She didn't get killed like her uncle, she killed her uncle and then came here, stopping off to kill on the way. You just saw it, didn't you? You saw the creature you've been saying doesn't exist.'

'I saw it too,' said the uniformed cop. His eyes were darting about nervously.

Schenk snapped at him, 'Shut up! I told you to arrest him.' Coming forward, Schenk was full of fury and accusations. 'What I saw, was you aiding and abetting two giants in costumes.'

'They didn't move like people in costumes,' argued the cop.

'I told you to shut up,' Schenk shouted without bothering to look at him.

More cars arrived in the road, visible half a mile away as their flashing lights bounced off the buildings.

The cop still hadn't moved, the three of us forming another stand off as clouds of breath drifted silently away above our heads. Schenk broke it when he stepped forward and tried to grab me. I slapped his hand away, a shocked look appearing on his face. The shock turned quickly to anger, which was never far from the surface or was always his first emotion, and he came at me again. The poor cop watched us, unsure what to do but certain he needed to do something. As I moved back again, he tracked me, his gun still pointing at the ground and his eyes glancing at the approaching cars, looking like he wanted them to get here sooner.

'You're under arrest, Otto Schneider,' Schenk sneered in my face with a smile teasing the corners of his mouth.

'I don't think so.' He reached for me again but this time I conjured air and hit him with a wall of it, pushing him off balance and then over as I hit him again.

He flailed briefly on the snow, struggling to get his feet back underneath his body. Then his face snapped around to look at me, nothing but a rage-filled grimace displayed as he went for his gun. 'You just assaulted a police officer.' He was getting up, his service weapon trained on my face but with a whisper I had an invisible barrier spell to hide behind.

'What are you talking about, Schenk?' I asked with a smile. 'I didn't touch you. Did I touch him?' I asked the uniformed cop. The poor man looked utterly bewildered.

Rescue for the younger cop came from the arriving cars, Chief Muller exiting the first of them. He needed about half a second to assess what he was seeing, and another second and a half to decide how he wanted to react. 'Schenk!' he bellowed.

Schenk didn't flinch, and he didn't take his eyes from me as he turned his face slightly to reply. 'Boss.'

'Put the gun down, Schenk. You're pointing it at an unarmed man.'

Schenk shook his head. 'Can't do that, boss. He is working with the killers. I saw it myself.'

Loud enough for everyone to hear, I said, 'You saw me confronting the beast, Schenk. There's just one of them and her name is Zuzana Brychta. She killed her uncle in Brno and has been killing ever since.'

'Put the weapon down, Schenk,' Muller repeated. 'I don't want to have to tell you again.'

'There were two of them,' Schenk roared, refusing to let go of his desire to take me down. I was bored already. My hands were getting cold too, held out to my sides and without gloves because I cannot spell cast with them on. Since they were free though, I drew from the nearest ley line, so when Schenk said, 'He's working with at least one of them.' I hit him with a tiny bolt of lightning.

I was aiming for his hand, my intention simply to spark him so he dropped his gun. The problem with lightning though is that is not exactly exact. So, I hit him in the head and dropped him like a stone.

Everyone saw me do it too. Not that I did anything which they could use for a conviction later; it wasn't like I made a gun with my finger and pointed it at him, I barely moved at all. Down he went though, a sea of surprised faces looking at him and then at me as Schenk's bladder emptied itself onto the cold ground.

Muller said some choice words as he lumbered across the snow. 'What the hell did you just do, Schneider?'

'Do?' I asked innocently. 'He got hit by lightning, you all saw it. I was standing here, I'm lucky it didn't get me as well.'

More choice words from the police chief because he knew I had done it and that he couldn't do anything about it. 'It's cold out here, Otto. It plays hell with my joints so why don't you cut the crap and tell me what Schenk thought he saw?' Then, he motioned to the uniformed cop who came with Schenk and those still up by the cars to get their fallen colleague off the snow. 'Put him back in the car and take him home.'

As his face swung back to mine, I started talking. 'I was tracking the girl. The one that went missing in Brno.'

'Zuzana Brychta? You said that she's the... werewolf.' He struggled with the last word as if it was uncomfortable in his mouth.

'That's right. Her signal led me here. Following it led me to the cathedral, which is where I got ambushed by a squadron of shilt.'

'Wait. That mess outside the cathedral is your doing?'

'I didn't say that,' I swiftly defended myself, sounding not even slightly convincing.

Muller gave me a raised eyebrow. 'You called them shilt. That's the name Nieswand used too.'

'It's what they are known as where they come from.' I saw the questions forming behind Chief Muller's eyes and held up a hand. Then I remembered how cold my hands were and dug in my pockets for gloves. 'There's so much to explain that will attack your sense of reality that I honestly don't think I should even start. Can I ask that you just accept some things?'

'Like what?' he growled.

'Do you remember that in Frau Weber's statement, when her daughter Katja went missing, she said there was a man in her room, and he created a pool of shimmering air behind him which he then stepped through and vanished? Several of your officers have reported seeing the same thing in the last week.'

'Yes. These reports have only started since you got involved.' He acknowledged that Frau Weber and others had made such reports, but he was reluctant to do so and then tried to deflect it onto me.

'The shilt can do the same thing: open a portal and step through it. I think a lot of the supernatural creatures we are dealing with can. They come from an alternate version of Earth.' He opened his mouth to ask a question, so I steamrollered on to stop him. 'You're about to ask why we haven't had this problem before. In truth, I don't really know all that much; I'm just piecing together bits of information. However, I believe something happened long ago which trapped them in the other place but now they are finding their way through.'

He waved a dismissive hand. 'Was Zachary Barnabus here? Tell me that.'

'Yes, he was. He appeared when I was fighting the shilt at the cathedral.'

'You know he's our number one suspect. Why weren't you fighting him? Or letting us know so we could make the arrest. Voss's men said... well they didn't say much because they are a tight-lipped bunch, but they said they tried to stop him, and you did nothing while he beat them up.'

I had to smile despite the seriousness of the situation. 'Okay, Chief. A couple of things. For starters, Zachary Barnabus hasn't done anything wrong; he is here to help. Second, he is an unstoppable, possibly invincible, shapeshifting werewolf who laughed when both Lange and Brubaker tasered him. A few days ago, I saw him get hit by a burst of hellfire from a demon. It should have killed him instantly, but he just got right on up again.'

Chief Muller heard the words hell fire and demon and once again struggled to bend his brain around the concepts. 'Schneider, I never know what you are making up and what might be true.'

I looked him dead in the eye, my voice imploring when I spoke again, 'You've seen what I can do, Chief. You don't want to believe it, but you know it's not a trick. I do magic.' He pulled a face. 'Let's just call it what it is. The Bureau have formed because they believe we have a growing problem with supernatural creatures. They see a war coming... or something,' I corrected myself when I saw the horror in the older man's eyes. I had been trying to tell him that Zuzana was the killer they were looking for but somehow I had gone off track. I started again. 'Zuzana Brychta is the killer. That's the thing I should have started with. I tracked her here expecting to find her body but hoping she might still be alive. Well, she's alive alright and leaving a trail of destruction in her wake. When Schenk turned up, she ran, and Zachary followed. That's what Schenk saw.'

'How do you know he isn't with her? You tell me they are both... werewolves,' he struggled to say the word again.

'You're asking me for proof, and I cannot give it to you.' He frowned at me. 'You have to decide whether to trust me or not. Either I'm a maniac with a bag of tricks, fooling everyone and helping killers for my own benefit. Or...' I left the word hanging while I pulled my gloves off. Then I summoned line energy and conjured just enough air to lift myself off the ground. Muller stumbled back a pace in shock. 'Or I'm a wizard and I am doing my best to defend the people of Bremen.'

I let myself back down lightly to the ground, glad I hadn't over done it and flipped myself into the frozen water behind me.

'How is this possible?' the chief murmured. He couldn't stop staring at me. I could never decide if showing people what I could do was a good idea, but no one had tried to dissect my brain yet.

I gave him my honest answer. 'I don't know. What I do know is that I am freezing, and I am exhausted, and I have had about two hours sleep in the last forty something. I am going home to rest; there's nothing more I can do here tonight. If you are going to arrest me, please get on with it and put me in a nice warm cell so I can get some sleep.' I really wanted to visit Kerstin in the hospital, conscious that my opportunity to visit her whenever I wanted would cease in a few days, and because I hadn't seen her last night. I knew I was too tired for it though, too tired and still too sick. If I went now, they would just bar me getting to her and most likely want to do more tests.

I genuinely think Chief Muller considered locking me up, just because it would make him feel better, but whether he decided he was happier with me on the loose to fight things he couldn't or figured I would escape the cell like Houdini, he said, 'You're free to go.'

'Thank you.' I had planned to go no matter what he said, but if I evaded the police and went home, they would just come for me there and disturb my slumber anyway. This was easier.

'I'm putting you back on the case too,' he added.

'And Heike?'

'She has her hearing tomorrow. I have to wait for that now.'

'You know it's a bunch of crap though. Prochnow was killed by a supernatural creature. Your service weapons, hell, any weapons you have, are useless against them. She couldn't have prevented his death no matter what she did. This is on you, Chief. I tried to warn you.' I was poking the bear again and he didn't like it.

A moment ago, I had been on my way home to bed, now I was in a fight again. He snapped at me, 'I can't tell the board that they have to let her off because some creature from hell is responsible.'

'Why not?' I snarled. 'It's the truth, isn't it?'

'You can't prove that, Schneider. And I can't change the way the system works.'

'No,' I scoffed. 'You're all going to keep bumbling along with your heads in the sand until something you don't want to believe in comes up and bites you.'

He started to fire a retort, but I was already walking away. I was cold and I hurt from the lack of sleep. Had I known what was waiting for me at my house, I would have slapped the chief's face and gladly spent a night in the cells.

Chapter 22

I managed to catch a tram and though it was cold on board with the constant opening and shutting of the doors, it was still far warmer than it was outside. I found a seat near one of the heater outlets and tried to warm myself. My hands were like two blocks of ice, the cold penetrating down to the bone to make them ache, but they began to thaw as I held them in the warm air.

The tram I was on didn't get me all the way home; I had to change at an intersection, waiting out in the cold again for five minutes until the tram I wanted came along. By the time I stumbled up to my door, I was half frozen again.

Fumbling for my key with unresponsive hands, I almost jumped out of my skin when a voice spoke to me. 'Herr Schneider?'

I whipped around, instinctively activating a barrier with a word as I prepared myself for yet another battle. I was even more shocked to find that no battle would occur. Waiting in the cold in the alcove near my front door where I kept logs for the wood burner was Katja Weber.

I lowered the barrier spell by murmuring the activation word again. 'Katja, what are you doing here?' Then I saw how cold she looked. The tiny teenager possessed no body fat to stave off the freezing temperatures and looked about ready to drop. Questions could wait. I got the door open and dragged her inside. 'We need to get you warmed up.'

I have underfloor heating right through the ground floor, which ensures the house stays warm. Katja needed more than that though. I had hold of her right arm by the elbow, pulling her through the house to the kitchen where I set the kettle to boil. I didn't drink tea very often, but always had some in case a guest wanted a cup. It would do for now.

Then I ran back to the log burner, opened the door and shoved in three pieces from the pile next to it. Pushing fire from my hand, I lit it and made sure it was burning, then grabbed a throw from the end of the sofa, wrapped the girl in it and sat her on the warm floor in front of the flames. She was shivering uncontrollably, and her lips were almost blue.

'How long have you been out there?' I asked.

Through chattering teeth, she managed, 'Two hours.' She was fumbling for her boots, trying to get them off but unable to grip them with her frozen fingers. Feeling very self-conscious, I gripped the fifteen-year-old girl's leg, the first time I had done that since I was a similar age and pulled off first one boot, then the next. Her feet were undoubtedly half frozen too and painful from it.

'Can you feel your toes?' I asked, concerned for frostbite. Her boots were made for fashion, not winter, the thin leather doing little to keep the cold out and she had leggings beneath her skirt but not the thermal kind.

'Not really,' she said, her teeth still chattering. 'They hurt.'

In the kitchen, the kettle clicked off. 'I'm getting us both some tea. While I do that, you need to get your leggings off, I want to check your toes haven't got frostbite. Let's warm you up and make sure I don't need to get you to hospital. Then you can tell me what you were doing outside my house in the middle of the night when it's ten below outside.'

I knew why she was here, of course. She wanted a teacher; she told me as much earlier. I saw it as both good and bad news. She needed a tutor for her abilities. It was that or quash them and pretend they weren't there. I had no idea what that would do but I doubted it was possible anyway, human curiosity would force her to investigate. So, in my opinion it was better that she have the chance to learn from someone like me; it would save her from the bruises, burns, spills and other adventures I endured as I tried to work things out for myself.

Of course, I was still learning myself, recent events having opened my eyes to what I could achieve but I thought I would, or, at least, could, be a good teacher for her. The problem that I was going to Daniel in a few days could not be avoided. If it was possible to return here when I wanted to, would I get the chance to train Katja? Would that attract more unwanted attention to her? I didn't know the answer to those questions.

I returned with two cups of tea, the bags still in the cups and steeping the water. 'Here. Try to sip it. Warming you up from the inside will work better.' She was sitting with her feet out in front of her, as close to the fire as she could put them without the heat being unbearable. They looked normal. From memory, frostbite affected areas look grey or blue and blisters would form when they warmed through again. Her toes just looked like toes.

After a few sips, she cradled the warm cup with both hands, holding it beneath her face so the steam warmed her. 'Thank you,' she said quietly.

I took a drink from my cup. 'Your parents don't know you are here, do they?'

She shook her head, a small reluctant movement. 'No.'

'You have to call them.' Her eyes darted across to meet mine, calling mum and dad was the last thing she wanted to do. 'Right now,' I added sternly. 'It is not okay for a fifteen-year-old girl to be in a man's house at this time of the night when they are not related.'

'I'm not a little girl,' she argued, her features betraying the hurt she now felt. 'Everyone treats me like I'm a little girl. I thought you would be different. Daddy got home this morning. He was so mad about the house. He was ranting about all the things he was going to sue you for. I told him it wasn't your fault and mum... mum said you rescued me and that it was the second time you had saved my life. He wouldn't have it. He just got more and more angry. I thought he was going to hit mum, so I did the thing with the air and threw him across the room.'

I closed my eyes. Was that my fault? I had shown her how to do it. 'What happened next?'

'I told him that I was like you. That I could do magic, and you were going to teach me. He stormed out and I ran away.'

This was bad. This was really quite bad. I got to my feet to get my phone. If she had been missing for hours in this weather, her mother, and her father, if he had returned, would be worried sick and calling all her friends to see where she had gone. Sooner or later they would check here, and I needed to have reported it first.

The moment I stood up I knew it was already too late. There were flashing lights playing off the trees outside. A heartbeat later, an insistent hammering started at my door. I hadn't even had time to fully warm up yet and I desperately wanted some sleep.

'Open up, Schneider.' The voice was authoritative and expected to be obeyed; a cop then. That went with the flashing lights, but I gave myself enough time to grab my coat again because I knew how much cold air was about to rush in.

I opened the door, a warm smile fixed to my face, but two cops barrelled past me, pushing me out of the way as they forced their way into my home.

I had time to shout an indignant, 'Hey!' before I heard a voice I knew.

Herr Weber was with them. 'Search the place,' he commanded as if they were his personal police officers.

'She's here,' one shouted from my living space.

'She was on my doorstep when I got back,' I protested. I was angry at the intrusion and the silent accusation.

Herr Weber ran inside to find her. I really wanted to stop him; he had no right to expect entry but stopping him now would start a fight and I didn't need that either. Unfortunately, I hadn't thought things through, so Herr Weber got to the living space in time to see his teenage daughter putting her leggings back on and jumped to a stupid conclusion.

Consumed by rage, he threw a punch at my face as I got to the top of the steps leading up from my front door. My instinctive spell threw him back across the room, but the cops hit me with a taser each and I don't remember what happened next.

Chapter 23

It was my belief that getting tasered puts you on your ass for a few minutes, but recovery is fairly quick. I don't know if it was the fatigue that did it, but I woke up four hours later. At the time, I didn't know how long it had been, I just knew it was much later.

I was in a cell. Initially disorientated, I sat up and scratched my head as the memories started to flood back. I felt better, that was something. I was warm for the first time in a while and I had slept though I felt quite groggy from it.

Being in jail wasn't doing me or anyone else any good so it was time to get some attention. I crossed to the bars and looked out, left and right. There was no one in sight. Much like the cell block where I was held in Berlin, all I could see opposite was a brick wall running left and right. I brought up my second sight and used it to check around. I was still in Bremen; I could see the big ley line, the one that runs alongside the river and past the cathedral. I often used it to orientate myself, so it was a relief to see it now.

'Hey,' I called to get attention. There was no reply. 'Hey,' I tried again a little louder.

From my left came a grumbling reply, 'Shuddup. I'm trying to sleep.' There was at least one other prisoner here then.

Ignoring his *polite* request, I pestered him for answers, 'How do I get the cops to come?' No answer came back, my inmate perhaps hoping I would 'shuddup' if he ignored me. 'I'm just going to keep asking until you tell me.'

My threat worked, the man in the next cell jumping off his bed with fast feet to run at the wall between us in rage. 'When we get out tomorrow, I'm gonna kill you,' he roared as the wall shook from his impact.

Thinking that a very unlikely outcome, I said, 'Yes, that's lovely. Now, how do I attract a police officer to come to my cell, please? I need to get out.'

This time a hand snaked around the wall and gripped the first bar of my cell. The hand was enormous, and all the knuckles were scabbed and bleeding. 'You either stop talking or I'm going to find out if I can come through this wall.' He made a fist with the hand I could see and then fell silent again, the hand retreating and the sound of him getting back onto his bunk letting me know the conversation was over so far as he was concerned.

I didn't bother asking him again. Not because I felt intimidated, but because he had made enough racket to attract a cop if one was going to come. They would be watching us on a screen somewhere and would be along when they felt like it.

Apparently though, they had been waiting for me to wake up because the very next second, I heard a door open and footsteps approaching. My inmate friend with the large hands had some choice words to say about the situation, but I stood at the front of my cell for whoever it was to arrive.

I was not happy to see Herr Weber. He was with a man I had seen in passing in the station. He was someone senior, but I hadn't learned his name, and they were both flanked by what looked to be a lawyer.

The cop spoke first, 'I'm Deputy Chief Peter Faulk. I believe you know Herr Weber, and this is his attorney Mattias Schweiger.'

'What am I charged with?' I got straight to the point.

'Attempted rape of a minor,' Faulk replied.

All I could do was stare at them. The cop had seen it all before. He was in his fifties, wearing a few extra pounds around his middle and looked like he smoked fifty a day. His hair was greying from the temples upward and he wore the trousers of a cheap suit, the jacket no doubt discarded in an office somewhere. His shirt was old and a little wrinkled and it had an old spaghetti sauce stain on it. In contrast Herr Weber and his attorney were wearing suits that probably cost the same as a family car. That didn't bother me. It was the smug look on Herr Weber's face that got me riled up.

'I saved your daughter,' I snarled at him.

'So, you claim,' he replied calmly. 'So, she claims too, actually, but as a minor her testimony has to be considered with an expectation for the fanciful. You gave her hallucinogenics or drugged her with something. For all I know, when she went missing last week, you had her all along. You have been grooming her, filling her head with nonsense and putting on fake pyrotechnic displays to augment your fantasy so you could seduce her. Seduce my fifteen-year-old daughter.' He made his voice shake at the horror of the idea as he said the last few words. It was a horrific idea, but he didn't know about my ability to hear lies and that was all I could hear from him. He knew nothing he said was true and he didn't care.

'All this?' I asked. He stared at me in question. 'All this just so you don't have to accept the truth that your little girl is different.'

'You've convinced her that she is a witch,' he roared, unable to keep his anger in check.

'I haven't done anything. I had never heard of her, or you, for that matter, until a few days ago when a demon came to your house to take her because of what she can do.'

'Another of your paedophile friends! It's a whole ring we have uncovered. How many of you are there?' His attorney touched his arm and whispered something quietly. Herr Weber nodded, straightening down his suit jacket as he forced himself to be calm. 'I am friends with the mayor. You should get used to your view; I doubt you will ever have another one.' Then he turned and left, his threat delivered.

The deputy chief lingered a moment longer. 'You are entitled to a phone call now you are awake. You'll be formally charged in the morning. The chance of bail is zero before you ask, suspected paedophiles never get let out, for their own safety as much as the community's. You want to make that call?'

I was having some trouble keeping my rage in check, but the deputy chief was just doing his job. I was going to leave this cell shortly regardless of what anyone thought. Chief Muller might have been more cautious with me, but Schweiger was buying Herr Weber's bullshit and saw no threat.

'No, I don't need to call anyone,' I told him quietly in a defeated voice.

He nodded once and left, taking a packet of cigarettes from his pocket as he went down the corridor.

Chapter 24

I found it ridiculous that I was thinking about how to break out of my cell. It had been what? Five days since I last broke out of one. Who needs to break out of jail that regularly?

My inmate friend's hand appeared around the edge of my cell again. 'I heard what they said. You're a kiddy-fiddler. I'm gonna enjoy killing you when we get out.' He made a fist with his hand again and pointed a meaty finger at me to make his point.

'My dear fellow, had you been paying closer attention, you would have heard the deputy captain assure me that I am not, in fact, getting out.'

'Gonna kill you anyway,' he promised and then started thumping on the wall, trying to beat his way through it as if that was supposed to scare me. Then he stopped and said, 'Do you know what I'm in here for?'

I gave his question a second of thought. 'Illegally impersonating the Easter Bunny out of season?'

I guessed wrong it seemed as his attempt to smash his way through the wall started again with renewed vigour and a lot more cussing, most of which was to do with performing an improbable act on me which involved a marrow. I let him get on with it, figuring he would tire himself out, throw a tizzy, and go to bed like a toddler might.

All my defensive rings were missing, taken from me when they brought me in no doubt. I felt a little violated that they had gone through my pockets and taken my things, but I had to acknowledge that it was an insignificant worry given some of the other obstacles I faced.

Ignoring my angry colleague, I focused on drawing line energy. There was plenty of it to be had in Bremen, so I drew in what I wanted, pulling more and more as I felt out into the earth to detect the walls. As luck would have it, the wall at the back of my cell wasn't an outer wall. Thinking about it, that would be a poor design and just encourage people to escape, so it made sense that we were tucked away deep inside the police station. Feeling around, I stopped when I found someone with a supernatural aura. They were above me, inside the station and not moving. I wondered if they might be a cop and whether they were aware of their supernatural abilities.

Pushing my curiosity to one side, I focused on the concrete where the bars of my cell sunk into the floor. Was it better to attack them or the lock? The lock seemed simpler, but as I began to pull moisture from the air, the crazed inmate did something I hadn't expected and managed to crack the mortar running between the bricks in the dividing wall. If he kept it up, he would come through. If he got through and my door was open, he would then be able to escape and cause havoc.

With a sigh, I refocused on the wall. I didn't know what he was in for, but it was unlikely to be illegally impersonating the Easter Bunny out of season. Even years after setting and drying, mortar still contains moisture. Not much, but sufficient for me to find it with a water spell. I focused on a small area, just the mortar around a couple of bricks where he was already starting to come through. Forcing cold into it, I froze the cells which caused them to expand, which, in turn, helped the mortar to crack.

My friend next door was coming through and I was helping him. When the first brick crashed out of its hole and broke in two on the floor, his face peered through at me, his piggy eyes masked by sweat from the effort.

I gave him a pinky wave.

In return, I got a bellow of rage and he started again, shoving his hand through the hole to grab the next brick and yank it free. He was a brutish ox of a man, lots of fat but plenty of muscle beneath it. He reminded me of wrestlers from my youth when the men on Saturday television were heavy rather than lean and powerful. They were incredibly strong, yes, but nowadays one had to look the part as well. All the American wrestlers; the ones making it into films and such, looked more like body builders than the wrestlers I grew up with.

He was coming through anyway, so I leaned on a wall and nonchalantly picked at the dirt under my nails. When he stopped for a breather, I said, 'Let me know if you need a hand.'

Further enraged by my lack of fear, he started kicking at the bricks. I figured I had ten seconds or so before the gap was wide enough for him to get through. 'Say your prayers, paedo,' he snarled between gulps of air.

He was big but he wasn't fit. The effort of getting to me had worn him out and he was gasping for breath. Taking advantage of that, I did something I hadn't done in a long time. As the next brick came free and he could get to me, I stopped the air in his lungs. I did it just as he tried to draw another huge breath in readiness to charge at me.

It was almost comical watching him try to breathe in and have nothing happen. Two seconds was all it took for the panic to set in, at which point he changed his desire to kill me and begged for help, pointing to his back and gesturing that I should perform the Heimlich manoeuvre. I gave it just a few more seconds, then leaned toward and blew gently on his forehead. He toppled to the right as his eyes rolled back and then I released the spell. As an afterthought, I made sure his chest was rising and falling.

Why hadn't I thought of using this before? I could have harmlessly subdued Zuzana at the park when I first saw her and that would have been that. I had to get out now. I knew how to find her, I just needed her panties back, preferably along with my compass. Both had been taken along with everything else in my pockets but would be in the station somewhere. Being trapped in a police station with my things locked away somewhere made my task more complicated, but hopefully not impossible.

I drew on the ley line again, conjuring moisture from the air to infiltrate the lock. This was the point at which I realised how dumb I had been. I waited for the ox to break through so he couldn't escape, but unless I put the lock back together, I had wasted my effort in knocking him out. He would come around soon enough and find my door open, plus any subsequent doors I needed to break through to get out. If I had just left while he was still in his cell, he might have stayed where he was.

It was too late to do anything about it; the door at the end of the hallway clanging as someone came through it. This time the footsteps weren't calm and unhurried, they were fast and flustered. The cops must have seen the ox break through the wall and finally gotten off their butts to respond.

'What the hell?' asked the first as he skidded to a halt at my cell door. He was staring at the ox on the floor, breathing steadily but very much unconscious.

Two more cops joined the first, staring down at the devastation that was our cells. 'How are you still alive?' asked one of them, a lean, blonde woman with brown eyes. 'We saw him break through and figured he would kill you.'

I smiled at her. 'Haven't you heard? I'm a wizard.' They clearly hadn't heard of me and didn't know what to make of my comment, but the ox chose that moment to wake up, so they were all about opening my cell and dealing with him.

All I got was a swift, 'Don't move,' when I stepped out of their way. The ox was getting to his feet and sleep had done nothing to dissipate his rage. He got one foot under his body, which was enough for him to propel himself upward to attack the first cop as he closed in. A giant hand knocked the poor man straight through the hole and back into the ox's original cell.

The batons came out and a lot of yelling ensued as I stepped lightly out of my cell and along the hallway to the door at the other end, pushing a spell into the locked door as I went. The cop had told me not to move but I figured it was a suggestion rather than an order given the circumstances.

The lock on the door popped as I used water to short out the keypad controlling it. I was out of the cell block bit of the station. All I needed to do now was find my things.

As I turned a corner, a voice from behind me said, 'Where do you think you're going?'

Chapter 25

I froze momentarily until my brain told me the voice belonged to Klaus Nieswand. As I spun around, I saw how worried he looked. 'What's up, Klaus?'

'You're supposed to be in a cell,' he hissed. 'That's why I'm down here. I came back in just a few minutes ago, Schenk's got us all working double shifts until we catch the killer, but when I got in I heard you had an altercation with him and tried to kill him and then they caught you with a child at your house. Is that right, Otto?' He looked like he didn't want to believe it, but had heard it from everyone in the station as the rumour mill kicked in.

'The girl was Katja Weber. She was at my house when I got there and frozen half to death. The charges against me are all her father's idea. As for Schenk, he was being a dick, so I hit him with a little arc of lightning that turned out to be not so little.'

Now looking relieved, Klaus asked, 'Why was she at your house? Is she running from Daniel?'

'Yes and no, I guess. Daniel assured me that he wouldn't come for her, but we had a fight in Magdeburg so I can't be sure what he might do now. She wasn't running from him tonight though; her abilities have come. I think they came a while ago.'

'Her... you mean she's like you? A wizard? I guess that makes sense. Daniel told us at the farmhouse we were all gifted with something.'

I dropped my second sight into place, seeing Klaus's aura for the first time. Why hadn't I noticed it before? 'You have it too, Klaus. I can see the ley line energy lighting you up.

Were you upstairs a few minutes ago?' I asked, thinking about the aura I had seen above me.

'Yeah. At my desk. Why?'

'Have you ever had a strange experience where you were able to do something you didn't think possible?'

He gave me odd look, like I was really going mad this time, but said, 'Well, there was the time I pulled Marian Svenson. Everyone said that was a miracle because she is so far out of my league.'

I shook my head. 'Not quite what I meant.'

'Look, we can't hang around here. What I ought to be doing is putting you back in one of the cells,' he held up a hand to stop me before I could speak. 'I know that wouldn't work though. How about I just get you out of here so you can catch the killer and I can stop pulling double shifts and get some sleep?'

'I need my things. Where will they be?'

Klaus glanced about, checking the coast was clear but just then the alarm went off; the cops in the cells must have secured the ox and then realised I was no longer there. He grimaced. 'That just made things harder.' He grabbed my arm, pulling me along the corridor. 'Quick, in here.'

I complied, because getting out of the station without anyone being hurt, including me, depended on Klaus right now. He was going to find a safe route and get me my things, two tasks I would find difficult without his help.

'Stay here. I'll be as quick as I can.' He opened a door and ushered me inside.

'It's a broom cupboard,' I pointed out, because, well, for one thing, it was a broom cupboard, but for a second, slightly more important reason, I wasn't going to fit.

Boots were coming down the hall around the corner and they were running. Klaus swore, grabbed some of the things from inside and shoved me in. As the door closed, I heard someone shout, 'Hey, Nieswand, you see anyone else down here? There's an escaped detainee.'

'Escaped?' he questioned. 'How the hell did someone escape?'

'It's that magician Schenk has been complaining about. He pulled some kind of switcheroo on the cell team and got out. Keep an eye out for him.' Then I heard the person pause. Most of the boots had faded into the distance but the person speaking had stayed behind. 'Why are you holding all the cleaning gear?' the voice asked, his tone dripping with suspicion.

Oh, nuts. I was going to get caught hiding in a broom cupboard.

Mercifully, Klaus was thinking on his feet. 'I'm not well,' he said, making a convincing gagging noise. 'I threw up around the corner. I need to clean it up. It's too awful to leave it for the cleaning crew.'

I heard someone's feet move, the other man backing away I guessed. He muttered some words of encouragement and was gone, following his colleagues and getting away from the sick person.

The door opened again, Klaus sagging against the frame. 'I thought we were busted then for sure.'

'Get my things. We need to get moving.'

He pushed himself upright, frowning at me. 'Alright, Bossy Pants.' He shut the door again. 'I'll be as quick as I can.'

As quick as he could felt like ages. I had no idea of time though until he returned. I heard feet hurrying along the hallway and assumed it was him, but since I couldn't tell, I had a handy air spell conjured and ready to throw at whoever was outside. I dropped it when his face appeared in the widening gap.

He had a plastic carrier bag with my things stuffed in it. 'It's pandemonium up there. The chief is back; they woke him up I think, and he is going nuts. He doesn't believe the attempted rape charge they have against you either. Apparently, he spoke with Frau Weber and Katja. Too late now though, you already broke out and I think Herr Weber has enough clout to cause you problems no matter what the chief thinks.'

'I've got a couple of days left here, Klaus. Then, unless I can find a very clever way out of it, I am going to be Daniel's pet, and no one here will be able to touch me.'

'That's the spirit,' he said, clapping me on the shoulder. 'Always find the silver lining.'

That wasn't what I meant but I let it go. As I stuffed things in my pockets; the compass in my back left, my wallet in the back right, Zuzana's panties in my front left, Klaus was leading me to a non-descript door which led in turn to a set of stairs.

'I think we can get out this way,' he told me as we went up. 'They already set guards at every exit; certain you are inside. Say, you can't do invisibility, can you?'

I rolled my eyes. 'No, Klaus. I don't think anyone can.'

'Hey, you're the one throwing magic around, I just thought I'd ask.'

'Klaus, how are we going to get out if they have all the exits blocked?'

In response to my question, he said, 'Aha!' an index finger in the air.

I waited for more. None came. 'Aha? What, Klaus, does, "Aha" mean?'

All I got in response was some well-waggled eyebrows. He led me up to the next floor, where, on the landing, he had two police issue coats, plus hats, gloves and other gear. 'We're going out in a cruiser.' He told me. 'Put your sunglasses on.'

Inside the hat were a pair of mirrored sunglasses. Where the hell had he found these? The eighties? Then he offered me a toothpick to put between my teeth.

'It's a disguise, okay? Just pretend you're Magnum P.I. He always looked cool in mirrored sunglasses while chewing a toothpick.' I thought he had his TV characters jumbled up but now wasn't the time for a discussion. He pulled on his coat and grabbed his radio. 'Central, this is five-eight-one-zero, receiving?'

A female voice came back instantly, 'Control. Go ahead.'

'I have a confirmed sighting of Schneider near the university on Hochschulring. He's with Barnabus, I think. I'm moving in for a closer look. Send back up.'

'Roger, five-eight-one-zero, proceed with caution.'

'Won't they know that's you?' I asked. He had given them a location two kilometres from where we were. I just had to hope it wouldn't turn out to be where we wanted to go. I hadn't activated the tracking spell yet and Zuzana could be anywhere.

'No,' he giggled, 'I gave them Bauer's number. He's a total dick. Now keep your head down and walk fast. There's a car right across from this door. Get in the passenger side and look like you belong. We are going straight out the door.'

It happened like clockwork or as if we had rehearsed it ten times. The door led into a garage area where cars were loading up and firing out, all of them off to catch me presumably. No one looked in our direction at any point as we crossed the concrete floor and slid into the police cruiser, Klaus unlocking it at the last moment.

The engine was running before my butt hit the seat and we were moving before I got my seat belt on. In the quiet of the car, once we were outside and I had the stars above me again, I asked, 'Won't you get into a whole lot of trouble for this?'

'Hell yeah. I took a look at my psychiatrist report yesterday though; she thinks I'm nuts. Cognitive Reasoning Disorder was what she listed it as, but she insisted I should tell her the truth about my two days in the immortal realm and then listed me as bonkers because I believed it was real. She recommended I be placed on administrative leave until I can be fully assessed and either retired or fixed.' Our eyes met across the central divide of the car. 'It's okay, I was thinking about quitting anyway. There're too many idiots like Schenk with altogether too much power. I might head back to school and study to be a veterinarian instead.'

I wasn't sure what to say to that, so I patted his shoulder in a brotherly way and focused on performing a tracking spell. 'How about we catch the killer?

'Hell yeah. Let's do that!'

Chapter 26

Among the other possessions returned to me was my phone. It told me the time. My eyes bugged out. 'Is it really five in the morning?'

Klaus glanced at the clock on the dash. 'Very nearly, yes. You sound surprised.'

'I am. When I got tasered it wasn't even eleven.' I had slept. Which explained why I felt better. Thinking about how I felt, I looked at my right hand again. The skin was slightly pink but that was all. The terrible burns and blackened flesh, the scabs that came after it were all gone, miraculously healed. Feeling inside my coat to the wound in my shoulder, I already knew I wasn't going to find anything. Now was the first time I had thought about it since I woke up so there was no surprise when I prodded the wound site and felt no pain or discomfort.

I still didn't know what to make of it, but a worrying thought had crept quietly into my head and was whispering things to me that I didn't want to hear. The tracking spell was pulling us back in the direction of the docks, past old town and the sight of the shilt battle just a few hours ago. As we passed it, I looked out of my window to the ruined plaza; there were dozens of people there and the whole area was cordoned off. There had been no reports of the demons killing anyone. The police had been racing to that location as Zachary and I escaped it, and the logical conclusion I drew was that the demons and angels (I couldn't think what else to call them) had returned to the immortal realm before anyone else arrived.

It was yet another thing I didn't really have time to dwell on.

'Do you think it's too early to call Heike?' I asked, intending to do it anyway but wanting his opinion so he could share the blame.

'Um, you get to call her Heike and phone her in the middle of the night. To me she is Lieutenant Dressler and I get kicked in the pants if I disturb her.'

I doubted that was actually true, but it made me smile as I dialled her number. It was answered instantly, Heike sounding like she was doing three things at once. 'Otto. I thought you were in a cell.'

'I was,' I replied carefully. 'Now I am not. How did you know?'

'I got a call from one of the guys at the station. I have friends there you know. They let you go?'

'Heike, I learned to fly this week. Walking through walls should be easy, right? Listen,' I said quickly before she could ask another question. 'I found Zuzana.' I wanted to catch her up because I knew she would have missed the news while sleeping.

'He didn't tell me that.' He probably didn't know. 'Was she dead?'

She wasn't hesitant when she asked the question like most people would be, the harsh realities of her job numbing her to the constant loss of life. 'No, Heike. Zuzana is the werewolf.'

She said a bad word. Then I heard her cooing in the background, her voice distant but sounding like she was talking to a dog. 'Sorry,' she said when she came back on the line. 'My youngest is sick. I've been up half the night.' That made me feel sorry for her, though she had got some sleep in the car yesterday evening. 'She's the killer, huh? That explains why they didn't find her in Brno and why she wasn't killed like every other victim.' She was quiet for a few seconds. 'She started with her uncle.'

'Yes, I have been thinking the same thing. I can't help wondering if there was a reason for it rather than she transformed and just went berserk. I spoke with her last night; there was no remorse for her actions, and she has no intention of stopping.'

From the driver's seat, Klaus got my attention, asking me if he should go straight on or turn at the next intersection. I checked quickly, indicating with my free hand that he should keep going. We were still heading for the docks, back to where she had been spotted once before.

Heike asked, 'Are you looking for her now?'

'Yes. I need something to use to get her on side though, some piece of information I can use. Can you call her mother? I'm going to try to talk her down, but I don't want to mention her mother if the relationship she had with her was less than amicable. Same thing with the father and the uncle. Maybe she has a sibling; there were family pictures on the wall in the kitchen that showed two girls. It might have been a childhood friend, but the other girl was a couple of years older, so I think it was an older sister who moved out.'

'I'll do what I can,' she replied. 'How long have I got?'

We were coming up on the docks, 'Ten minutes?'

She laughed at me. 'Sorry, I was just laughing at how ludicrously easy this is. I was expecting a challenge.' Her flippant reply summed up our situation nicely.

I started to apologise but she had already hung up; time was not our friend. I had a terrible itch inside the back of my skull. To our knowledge, she had killed nothing but men since leaving Brno, targeting men associated with the sex industry and taking out one lowlife after another. There was one exception: the girl in Prague. I worried to find out who she was.

The compass swung suddenly as Klaus hit Hafenstrasse. 'Stop the car.'

He pulled to a stop and looked across at me. 'Is she here?'

'Somewhere close by. I go the rest of the way on foot.'

'We go.'

I pursed my lips and swivelled around in my chair to look at him. 'You're not coming with me, Klaus.'

'But.'

'It's too dangerous. I probably shouldn't be doing this either, but you definitely have to circle around and pretend you were never here. I'd make it an order if I could.'

'I can help. Maybe if we catch a werewolf, I can prove I'm not nuts. I'd like to see the psychiatrist dispute a live werewolf doesn't exist when it's right there in a cell.'

'You're not coming,' I repeated, my tone more forceful. 'I can't fight her and watch out for you. It's likely to get both of us killed.'

He looked a little sulky, but when I patted his shoulder again and opened the door, he made no attempt to follow me. Once out, I tapped the roof of the car and he pulled away, doing as I asked, thankfully.

'I figured you'd be here sooner or later,' said a Zachary shaped shadow as it stepped away from a wall. I'd spotted him with my second sight as soon as we came into the street, the line energy powering his transformation glowing brightly in the dark.

'Do you know where she is?' I asked.

'In an apartment on the second floor. The whole building stinks of death. Honestly, I'm surprised you can't smell it too.' I didn't have werewolf senses and I couldn't smell what he was smelling, not that I was sure I would recognise the smell of death.

My brow winkled as I thought of a question. 'Why did you wait for me?'

'She ran from me last time because she saw me as a threat. I want to show her that I am not. I knew you would track her again and I didn't want to convince her to come with me and then run into you with a bunch of cops. She would think I had walked her into a trap and would never trust me again. That's why I waited.'

I knew what he wanted; I just didn't see how it could possibly happen. 'She can't leave with you, Zac. She's killed a bunch of people. Ripped them to shreds and robbed them. She's not going to stop.'

'You don't know that, Otto.'

I hung my head. This was an impossible argument to win. 'What are you proposing? To take her away from the city and rehabilitate her?'

I could see that Zachary was angry, with the situation more than me, I thought, though it could be the pressure of being in the city causing the upset. 'She deserves a chance. The people she killed were all assholes.'

'She killed a girl in Prague.'

He didn't have a reply for me, except to say, 'No magic.'

'What?'

'No magic, Otto. She's lashing out and hurting people because she is frightened, not because she is evil. I didn't wait here so you could attack her, even if your intention is to subdue rather than hurt. I'm here to make sure you don't do either.'

I blew out an exasperated breath. 'What if she doesn't give me a choice?'

'Can you subdue her without doing any permanent damage?'

I thought about the air spell I used on the ox. 'Yes, I think so.'

He pushed the door open and stepped inside.

Chapter 27

I trailed behind Zachary, unhappy about his plan to take Zuzana away. I would be happy to talk to her, to talk her down, if you like. It might make the fight I felt certain was coming less likely, but could I convince her to surrender herself into custody if Zachary was offering escape? I didn't think so and that meant I was going to have to fight both of them.

It wasn't a prospect I relished.

At the second-floor landing, Zachary pushed open a door to lead us into a dingy hallway. There was no light coming in from outside and the motion-triggered lights set into the ceiling were mostly broken. The ones that did work, illuminated a patchwork of graffiti and stains. I didn't want to think about the stains.

Zachary paused as if listening. 'You really can't smell that?' he asked.

I sniffed. I could smell plenty and none of it was nice, but it was just the smell of musty carpets, dirt and food waste. 'What am I supposed to be smelling?'

'Nevermind. It's probably best if you don't know.' He pointed to a door. 'This is the place.' He caught my quizzical expression. 'I can tell by the smell.' I sniffed again, still getting nothing. Until he opened the door, that is. The door was locked, which didn't present much of an obstacle for him. He just turned the handle anyway and gave the door a gentle shove. The frame splintered quietly enough, which is to say it didn't echo loudly down the hall, but there was an instant reaction from inside the apartment. I caught the smell as soon as I stepped inside.

'Zuzana we are not here to hurt you,' Zachary called out. 'Let me help you get to safety.'

The apartment was mostly a single room, with a couch and a TV. There was a kitchenette along one wall. The nineteen-year-old woman burst out of one of two doors I could see. It had to be her bedroom, the other door would be the bathroom and I could tell the smell was coming from there.

All she had on was a t-shirt. It covered what was necessary though only just, but she was already beginning to transform. Zachary rushed her, grabbing her arms and pinning them, far stronger than her since he was already in werewolf state.

'Don't change,' he begged. 'I'm your friend. Let me help you.'

She screamed in his face. 'No!'

My phone beeped, a message popping through and I felt certain it was from Heike. Yanking it from my pocket even with the drama unfolding across the room, I swiped the screen and got the answer I dreaded but also expected.

Zachary was doing his best to hold her in place and stop her from changing, but I could see it wasn't going to work. The more he tried to stop her, the more she would resist.

With a gentle voice, I asked, 'Why did you kill your sister?'

The question reached her ears and her thrashing to break free subsided as she looked at me. It wasn't guilt on her face though, it was venom. 'Because that bitch left me with him. She could have protected me. She could have taken me with her, but she ran away. Ran away and left him to focus all his attention on me.'

'Your uncle,' I confirmed. 'He abused you?'

Her cheeks coloured with shame she had no reason to feel. None of what happened at home was her fault, but it didn't change anything about what she had done since. 'I should have killed my mother as well. She knew about it, even though she pretended she didn't; she knew. I told her once when I was fifteen and she slapped my face. I wanted to go back to Brno to settle that score, but I'm never going back. Not now. And I'm not going with either of you.'

'You cannot stay here,' Zachary argued. 'They will catch you.'

She snapped at him, 'I don't think so. They can't get close, and do you know how strong I am?'

To interrupt her, I asked, 'What's in the bathroom, Zuzana?' I already knew the answer, it wasn't difficult to guess. She had only been here a few days and had an apartment filled with possessions like she had lived here for weeks.

'Some creep I met on the internet. Just like every other man, all he wanted was to screw me. People should be thanking me for the work I have done.' Zachary bowed his head as she spoke; he wasn't going to be able to talk her into changing what she had become.

I took a pace to the side so I could see inside and pushed the door open. I wouldn't claim to know much about decomposition but the naked man in the bathtub must have been in there for days now. And she was sleeping five metres away from it without the slightest concern.

She saw me look, saw the look of revulsion on my face and made her decision. An uppercut caught Zachary by surprise. Delivered as she was transforming, it carried enough power to lift him off his feet and give her the room she needed to escape. I whispered, 'Cordus,' to create a barrier but she wasn't going through me to get to the door; she ran two paces in the opposite direction and dived out of the window, smashing glass and letting the cruel air in from outside.

Zachary dived after her, never pausing to check for danger below. Staring at them from the broken window, I cursed myself for not taking her out when I had the chance. I should have cut off her air and ended it before anyone else could get hurt. Now I might lose her.

Zuzana hit the street below, her transformation complete, and started running instantly. The docks and the Weser river were just to her right as she ran up the centre of the deserted street with Zachary once again hot on her heels.

Seeing no choice but to follow them, I too jumped out of the window, doing my best to control my fall with a conjuring of air to cushion my landing. It almost worked, the lack of practice resulting in a heavy landing that stung both my soles. I hobbled after Zachary and Zuzana, pushing away the pain and cursing my weakness.

Running along the street, falling further and further behind the much faster werewolves, I jumped out of my skin when a police cruiser pulled alongside me. I didn't have time for this now, but just as I thought I was going to have to repel cops who thought I was an escaped criminal (okay, technically, I am), I saw it was Klaus at the wheel.

'Get in!' he yelled, matching pace with me.

I nearly argued, but I couldn't catch them without him. So, I got the rear door open and fell inside, inertia from acceleration instantly pinning my face to the seat back as he took off.

'I thought I told you to get clear,' I ranted with exasperation once I managed to right myself.

He shook his head. 'I had to come back. Someone spotted Zachary and reported it. There's a whole army of police and the goons from the Bureau heading this way. When they get here, they will catch you too. We have to get you clear.'

He was a good man, and he was putting himself not only in harm's way but also jeopardising his career and his freedom by helping me. Leaving the area might be the sensible option but I had left the jail to stop Zuzana because I doubted anyone else could; nothing about that had changed.

I grabbed the back of his seat to lever myself forward and pointed to the fleeing figures in the distance. 'Catch up to them.'

He didn't argue, thankfully, and was able to close the distance in a few seconds. We didn't catch them though because Zuzana heard us coming, glanced over her shoulder at the car and went vertical, scaling the wall of the dockyard to vanish inside.

Zachary went after her.

I swore and slapped Klaus on his shoulder. 'Pull it over. I'll go on foot.' As he hit the brakes and my face smooshed into the back of his seat, I managed to say, 'And for God's sake, get out of here this time.'

I bailed the second the car's forward braking inertia fell to a point where my muscles were strong enough to lever me upright again. A slap on the roof got Klaus moving once more, but I could hear sirens in the distance; I was going to run out of time soon.

There was no gate. That was my first problem. The stupid dock wall stretched both left and right as far as I could see, so, once again, I was going to have to try flying. Werewolf claws might grip brick, but my fingers wouldn't.

I really wanted to keep my gloves on; it was horribly cold this close to the river, but to conjure they had to be off. Feeling the cold on them the second they were exposed, I pulled on the ley line and pushed myself upward. Maybe one day I would work out how to do it gracefully, but this time, I got confused when I went over the wall. I failed to adjust for the change in comparative distance between what I was pushing down against, so as my downward force hit the top of the wall, it flipped me upside down and into the dockyard. I was too out of control and twisted in the air to work out which way was up. If I pushed air and got it wrong, I might power myself into the ground, so I dropped the spell, clenched my jaw, and braced for impact.

I hit the ground with my left shoulder, a shock of pain making me gasp. Half a second later, I hit the same piece of unforgiving ground with my head. A shout from somewhere above stopped me from wasting time on trivia such as agony. It was Zachary.

He was on a derrick with Zuzana. High above the dockyard, their figures silhouetted against the moonlit sky to send the dockworkers scattering. They could be anywhere else in the city and run into virtually no people, but no, we had to be at the dockyard where ships came in day and night regardless of the weather.

I could hear their conversation but not make out the words, mostly it was drowned out by the panicked escape of the derrick driver cussing and screaming as he attempted to descend his ladder at world record speed.

I wasn't going to try to fly up to them, missing the thin platform would just put me in the river where I would quickly freeze to death. I couldn't go up the ladder either because the driver was still only halfway down it. In the end, neither thing was necessary because Zuzana led Zachary into a trap. Whether she knew it was there or not in advance, as he followed along the arm of the derrick, climbing higher and higher, she reached down to grab a cable and gave it a yank.

It went taut as she pulled, whipping up to take out Zachary's legs. He fell from a height of at least forty metres, one clawed hand raking the steel of the derrick's arm to draw sparks, but it failed to find purchase and he tumbled into the river below.

He would survive, I felt certain of that, but he was out of the fight and would be swept swiftly downriver.

That left just her and me.

Chapter 28

Could I honour Zachary's request and take her alive? I didn't know but I conceded to give it one try. She was descending the derrick, climbing down at speed as I drew in more energy from the ley line.

When she got to ten metres, she jumped the rest of the way and that was when I sent my first spell. Using air to catch her, much like I had tried to catch myself as I fell from flying, I held her five metres off the ground. She fought and writhed, but she had nothing to push against and no way to escape. If she had a weapon to fire or a rock to throw, I might be in trouble, but she didn't, so just like that, I had her.

Except I didn't.

My mental victory dance was short-lived as she ripped out a ten-centimetre-long claw and threw it at me. I was too surprised to raise a barrier that might have saved me and too dumb to duck or dodge it. The black dagger-like claw hit me high on my left, sinking into my pectoral muscle by at least five centimetres. I howled in pain and could not maintain the spell.

As I stumbled backward, grasping at my chest to remove the claw, she landed nimbly just a few metres away and spread her arms to show me the other nine claws.

I sat up to conjure my next spell, grunting, 'I tried, Zac. I really did.' I was done with playing nice, now it was time to try to save my own life. As she hunched her legs and came for me, diving with her claws leading, I used air to shove me backward out of her grip and then I hit her with lightning. I didn't have much time to build it up but even a small bolt of lightning will put most things down.

It lit her up from the inside, arcing and fizzing over her body and making her contort as her muscles spasmed involuntarily. She didn't go down though. It made her pause, but as soon as the blast dissipated, she was coming for me again.

I hit her with more lightning. Harder this time and kept the lightning on her as I clambered to my feet. Even as the electricity coursed through her and must have been agony to endure, her eyes were focused on mine, pure hatred in them and nothing else.

Backing up a step as the lightning vanished into the ground, I wondered how much she could take. Just like Zachary, she seemed impervious to all forms of attack. Not only that, each of my attacks was just making her angrier.

She started forward yet again, and I knew I was going to have to try something seriously drastic if I hoped to stop her. Fire would hurt her, but in all likelihood, it would do little more than piss her off. Air would tickle and maybe throw her about a bit but was a delaying tactic at best. That left water and earth and a few dirty tricks.

She came again. Stalking toward me with an evil glint in her eyes, she licked her lips meaningfully. She was certain I stood no chance and was going to prove it by eating me. Conjuring air in my terror, I felt into her body with my senses and shut off the air to her lungs. I could have picked a water spell and tried to kill her from the inside like I had with Teague, but I still wasn't certain what that experience had done to me. This, I believed, would render her unconscious in under a minute. There was a part of me that wanted to kill her; she was like a rabid beast, too dangerous to be left alive. I wasn't a killer though, not if I could help it. This wasn't like taking the life of a shilt, a creature who existed just to drain the life from humans. Underneath her snarling, muscle-bound frame, was a nineteen-year-old girl who had been dealt a raw hand.

She gagged, her eyes bulging out as I starved her body of the oxygen it needed. Faltering, she placed a hand on the ground just as the sound of the approaching sirens grew significantly in volume. I didn't turn to look, but the flashing lights went by in the street behind me, red and blue bouncing off every surface. They would have to go to the dock entrance and then work their way through the dock to find us, but the net was closing in. Above all else, I needed to make sure she was unable to attack them before they arrived. With her in my custody, I could argue the necessity of the jail break, not that it would matter much when I went with Daniel. More than that though, she would tear them to shreds if she could, so I held the spell on, depriving her body of the air it so badly craved.

Then she leapt. It was a last-ditch effort, her final roll of the dice before the blackness took her, but she was a natural killer and came forward with both hands extended. An air spell would have pushed her away, deflecting her in mid-flight but I was already using an air spell and there was no time to drop it for another.

The shock of her knife-like claws puncturing my chest was unbelievable. It was the most incredible switch because now it was I who couldn't breathe. My lungs were like two teabags, perforated multiple times and though she was gasping for breath, my spell had dropped, and she was going to win.

'You should have left me alone when I told you to,' she growled, her breath hot on my face she was so close.

Staring down at her hands, each of them buried to the fingertips in my rib cage, I felt a sense of detachment. It was done. I had lost and there was nothing I could do to stop myself from dying. My consciousness swam and as it did, my head lolled, and I saw the thing that would save everyone but me.

I didn't have a lot of energy left. But maybe I had just enough to end things properly. She was about to pull her claws out; I could see her muscles bunching and I doubted I could stay conscious when the next wave of pain hit me.

With my eyes firmly closed to calm myself, I focused on the ley line beneath me as it writhed in the earth. Then with all my might, I tore into the sky using air to lift me high above the cold ground of the dockyard. I carried her with me, my left hand gripping around her back to hold her in place. Then, I nudged us sideways and sent heat to the diesel fuel tank I had spotted. It was just sitting there on the dockside, filled and ready to refuel the vehicles.

It ignited as we plunged down to it, exploding outwards even as we fell through the middle of the expanding fireball.

I felt nothing.

Chapter 29

The explosion spat me out, shooting me along the ground to tumble and roll uncontrollably across the frozen dockyard. I had to shield my eyes as I sat up, and shuffle backward from the oppressive heat. My clothes were smouldering but not on fire, smoke rising from them as if they were just about to combust. My hands were steaming where sweat, or perhaps blood, was cooking off. There was no possible way I could be alive.

Yet I was.

My lungs were working too.

'What just happened, Otto?'

The voice startled me, not that it was the first time Daniel has snuck up on me, but I recognised that it was him without turning to look. When I didn't bother to answer, he said, 'I felt a change through our binding. It snapped and then reformed as if you had momentarily died. Whatever have you been doing?'

He moved around to stand in front of me and crouched to look at me from the same level. I scowled at him. 'Why are you here?'

'I just told you,' he said with some irritation. 'First you flee from Bremen and now I find you trying to break our binding, a magic you should not be capable of.'

I wasn't paying much attention to him. I was looking at the fire raging behind him as the diesel burnt and lit the sky. The tank must have been mostly empty otherwise there would be a lake of flames advancing across the dock. As it was, the lower half of the tank was still intact and was doing a good job of containing the fire. I focused on a point when I thought I saw something move, certain that Zuzana could not hope to survive the fire, but checking, nevertheless. A figure struggled to its feet. Unbelievably, she was still going. Just as I felt the need to ready another spell and wondering if I had the energy to do so, she collapsed again. I continued to watch but this time it was over.

I made a silent apology to Zachary.

Behind me the sirens were drawing ever nearer. Falling into the fire and surviving it had confirmed a sneaking suspicion; something I didn't want to admit to myself. I couldn't deny it now though, and it was time to renegotiate. Getting to my feet, I said, 'The deal we have needs to change.'

'You continually fail to grasp your position, Otto. We are servant and master. If you defy me, I will simply kill you and take Katja as I have previously threatened. If you disobey me, I will send the shilt to Bremen. I can torture you in ways you cannot imagine. It is far better for all parties if you conform as required. You made the deal and bound yourself to me. Choose now, I shall waste no more time discussing this subject. Conform or die?'

I shot him a wry smile and drew line energy in to power a spell.

Confused, he asked, 'What are you doing?'

'I'm choosing, Daniel. I choose to die.' Then I beckoned him with my outstretched left hand. 'Give it your best shot.'

His eyebrows twitched in a moment of surprise, his amused expression gone in a flash as he pushed hellfire into two orbs of pulsing dark red death and fired them both at me.

I wondered if it was going to hurt as I leaned in to take the blast. It did, much like getting hit by lightning as I felt all the cells in my body catch fire and then instantly return to normal. The energy shunted me back, but I used air to form a cushion to my rear. It kept me upright, like bouncing off a pillow and I smiled at Daniel once more.

Perturbed, he shot me again with the exact same effect, only this time I hit him back with lightning. I knew it wouldn't do much to him, but it wouldn't tickle either.

He took a faltering step back, his face unable to hide the stunned expression he wouldn't want me to see and I held my hands up once more as a threat. 'That immortal thing you have, Daniel? Well, it's catching.' His eyes were wide, but he threw neither of the hell fire balls he held. 'I can explain the how of it later. Right now, the police are coming, and we need to renegotiate our deal. Assuming, of course, you see some advantage to having an immortal wizard as your familiar. We can call the whole thing off if you wish.'

'You can't be immortal,' he stammered. 'It's not possible.'

I took a step toward him, getting close just as the cop cars squealed into the dockside area and were suddenly right on top of us. They saw me, their brakes slamming on. I heard at least one car bump another as they all tried to pull up in the small space.

Daniel shifted his stance to throw hellfire in their direction as they started to pile out of the cars. I slammed into him with my body, sending his shots wide as we grappled. 'No more humans will be killed here. No more humans will be taken as slaves for your demon kin. Bremen has a defender and he cannot be killed.'

'I'll find a way,' Daniel snarled into my face. He wasn't cowed at all. He knew he couldn't be hurt and that he could bring down what might be unlimited forces on my city if he chose. I was its self-appointed defender, but I couldn't be everywhere. He would get in and take people if he wanted to no matter what I did.

A loud hailer interrupted my thoughts. 'Otto Schneider. Lay down on the ground and surrender. You will not receive a second warning.' The sound of dozens of rifles being made ready accentuated his point. Perhaps they couldn't kill me, but then what? Weber had a trumped-up attempted rape charge against me. It wouldn't stick but it would cause me problems. He was already trying to sue me for attacking him with magic and I had escaped from a cell inside a police station. Guilty or not, they were going to make my life difficult.

'You have three seconds,' the voice assured me.

I looked square at Daniel. 'If I go with you, I want to be able to return here. I have a wife to visit and a student to train. I will work with you, not for you.'

'You will do my bidding,' he snarled.

'That's my deal, demon. You get an immortal wizard to help you, but Bremen is off limits and I get to return here when I want to.'

'You talk as if you have a choice, wizard. You are bound to me. It cannot be broken, and you will do as I command.' Then he spoke a word, 'Incensus,' and I felt all the effort leave my body. Suddenly I was a helpless rag doll, utterly unable to operate any of my limbs. Only my organs seemed to work. And my eyes, I realised, as he opened a portal and grabbed my collar. He could have done this to me at any point.

As someone shouted, 'Open fire!' he pulled me into the shimmering air and whispered. 'You have so much to learn, Otto.'

The End

Author Note:

H^{i there,}

As I close this book, the South of England where I live, in fact pretty much the whole of England, is being buffeted by a storm. I would happily hide in the house, but my writing space is in a log cabin at the bottom of the garden. I also have three dogs and a bunch of chickens so staying inside where it is warm and dry isn't really an option.

Drawing my four-year-old son's attention to the news and an article showing the devastation wrought across the country, he watched as storm waters swept a truck trailer away. I thought it was a neat demonstration of the power our planet can wield, and that tied in nicely to what I am currently writing. Hunter didn't get that though, he had an immediate solution to the problem, which was for the truck itself to go after the trailer by transforming into amphibious mode. Quite whether this came from watching Transformers cartoons, playing with Lego, or just his own imagination, I wasn't able to determine. I was content, though, to let him invent his own world; it's what I do all day after all.

This second book in the wizard series, set within The Realm of False Gods universe I have created, has allowed me to get my teeth into the story and where it is all going. In order to get to this point, I had to develop five series, each with their own characters and you can look forward to meeting all of them soon, assuming, that is, you have started with Otto and haven't arrived at him last. You may have read this book years after I wrote it. If you are an early reader, you will find the Otto story continues soon enough, in the meantime, because I have so much to share with you, Zachary has his own stories, and then you will meet Anastasia and then the sisters. Magic is sparking to life all over the mortal realm as the death curse weakens. It is not one sided though; the demons have a plan and so do the angels.

I need to end this here and get back to plotting the next stage because the cataclysm is coming and not even I have the power stop it.

Steve Higgs

Eccles, Kent

February 2020

More Books By Steve Higgs

Blue Moon Investigations
Paranormal Nonsense
The Phantom of Barker Mill
Amanda Harper Paranormal Detective
The Klowns of Kent
Dead Pirates of Cawsand
In the Doodoo With Voodoo
The Witches of East Malling
Crop Circles, Cows and Crazy Aliens
Whispers in the Rigging
Bloodlust Blonde – a short story
Paws of the Yeti
Under a Blue Moon – A Paranormal
Detective Origin Story
Night Work
Lord Hale's Monster
The Herne Bay Howlers
Undead Incorporated
The Ghoul of Christmas Past
The Sandman
Jailhouse Golem
Shadow in the Mine
Ghost Writer

Felicity Philips Investigates
To Love and to Perish
Tying the Noose
Aisle Kill Him
A Dress to Die For
Wedding Ceremony Woes

Patricia Fisher Cruise Mysteries
The Missing Sapphire of Zangrabar
The Kidnapped Bride
The Director's Cut
The Couple in Cabin 2124
Doctor Death
Murder on the Dancefloor
Mission for the Maharaja
A Sleuth and her Dachshund in Athens
The Maltese Parrot
No Place Like Home

Patricia Fisher Mystery Adventures
What Sam Knew
Solstice Goat
Recipe for Murder
A Banshee and a Bookshop
Diamonds, Dinner Jackets, and Death
Frozen Vengeance
Mug Shot
The Godmother
Murder is an Artform
Wonderful Weddings and Deadly
Divorces
Dangerous Creatures

Patricia Fisher: Ship's Detective Series
The Ship's Detective
Fitness Can Kill
Death by Pirates
First Dig Two Graves

Albert Smith Culinary Capers
Pork Pie Pandemonium
Bakewell Tart Bludgeoning
Stilton Slaughter
Bedfordshire Clanger Calamity
Death of a Yorkshire Pudding
Cumberland Sausage Shocker
Arbroath Smokie Slaying
Dundee Cake Dispatch
Lancashire Hotpot Peril
Blackpool Rock Bloodshed
Kent Coast Oyster Obliteration
Eton Mess Massacre
Cornish Pasty Conspiracy

Realm of False Gods
Untethered magic
Unleashed Magic
Early Shift
Damaged but Powerful
Demon Bound
Familiar Territory
The Armour of God
Live and Die by Magic
Terrible Secrets

About the Author

At school, the author was mostly disinterested in every subject except creative writing, for which, at age ten, he won his first award. However, calling it his first award suggests that there have been more, which there have not. Accolades may come but, in the meantime, he is having a ball writing mystery stories and crime thrillers and claims to have more than a hundred books forming an unruly queue in his head as they clamour to get out. He lives in the south-east corner of England with a duo of lazy sausage dogs. Surrounded by rolling hills, brooding castles, and vineyards, he doubts he will ever leave, the beer is just too good.

If you are a social media fan, you should copy the link below into your browser to join my very active Facebook group. You'll find a host of friends waiting there, some of whom have been with me from the very start.

My Facebook group get first notification when I publish anything new, plus cover reveals and free short stories, but more than that, they all interact with each other, sharing inside jokes, and answering question.

 facebook.com/stevehiggsauthor

You can also keep updated with my books via my website:

g   https://stevehiggsbooks.com/

Printed in Great Britain
by Amazon

39810191R00108